THE CASE OF THE POACHED PERIDOT

A Paranormal Cozy Mystery

B I Skinner

CONTENTS

1. Chapter 1 — 1

2. Chapter 2 — 5

3. Chapter 3 — 8

4. Chapter 4 — 11

5. Chapter 5 — 15

6. Chapter 6 — 18

7. Chapter 7 — 21

8. Chapter 8 — 24

9. Chapter 9 — 28

10. Chapter 10 — 31

11. Chapter 11 — 32

12. Chapter 12 — 37

13. Chapter 13 — 41

14. Chapter 14 — 44

15. Chapter 15 — 45

16. Chapter 16 — 49

17. Chapter 17 — 51

18. Chapter 18 — 55

19. Chapter 19 — 59

20. Chapter 20 — 63

21. Chapter 21 — 65

22.	Chapter 22	67
23.	Chapter 23	70
24.	Chapter 24	74
25.	Chapter 25	77
26.	Chapter 26	82
27.	Chapter 27	84
28.	Chapter 28	89
29.	Chapter 29	92
30.	Chapter 30	99
More Books by B I Skinner		101
Copyright		102

1

— • —

"Is this party a dud or what?" a ghost whispers in my ear, so suddenly I jump. His old-fashioned night gown tells me he died in the late 1800s. Maybe he was here when the Red Castle Hotel first opened.

Juliet, one of my dearest friends, a sun witch, and the owner of Sol Conceptions Bakery, laughs at my discomfort. "Did a ghost just say something to you?"

"Yes." I scowl, trying to swat him away.

"What did he say?" she asks.

"He said the party was a dud."

"He's got that right," Wendy grumbles, draining her third peppermint martini, then slamming the empty glass on the table with a resounding thud. "Another martini, barkeep!" she shouts to no one in particular.

"I think maybe you've had enough," I tell her with Juliet nodding in agreement. "Won't you have a pile of customers tomorrow, eager to spend their Christmas money on new books? You don't want to be all hungover and grumpy."

"Pssshhhh! What customers?" she asks.

Wendy is also a witch who owns the Looking Glass Bookstore at 6th and Maple.

It's one of many small businesses in Glenwood Springs suffering from a spate of bad luck. She's also among those who believe the bad luck results from the missing peridot. Last summer, someone stole a rare jewel affectionately known as the Precious Peridot from its enchanted display case at the Museum of Jewels and Gems.

Shortly after it went missing, Glenwood's mayor hired me to locate it. You see, I'm a Paranormal Private Investigator. I see dead people. Actually, I don't just see them; I also talk to them. No, not all of them. Just the ones who refused to go into the light.

They tell me it's blindingly bright and comfortingly warm at first, so most souls naturally gravitate to it. However, some are just too stubborn or think they're too busy to bother with it, so they stick around. The light fades over time, eventually disappearing altogether.

Spirit communicators like me are rare. As a young child, I assumed everyone saw ghosts. My parents just thought I had a lively imagination and liked to make up pretend friends.

But when I was six years old, my friend's grandma died. My mom baked a casserole we took to their house for the wake. When grandma approached me, I was with the rest of the kids in the backyard playing on the swing set. Grandma and I had a fascinating conversation.

She explained she couldn't go into the light until she told someone about the shoebox full of cash hidden under a loose floorboard in the attic. When I told the adults about my conversation with grandma and where she hid the money, my parents realized I was a ghost whisperer. The other adults assumed I must have overheard grandma talking about it at some point, but my parents knew what really happened.

They accepted my gift, but thought it was best not to tell anyone. They knew some people would want to exploit it while others might be afraid and try to harm me.

After *they* died, I went into foster care. I knew instinctively that I couldn't share my secret then. I was a kid in the system with ill-fitting hand-me-down clothes and lavender eyes, so I got bullied a lot. The few times I slipped up, and kids caught me talking to ghosts, they made fun of me for having imaginary friends.

If only they knew what the spirits were telling me about what happened in some of their homes! I knew exactly who drank too much, who was having an affair, and which pastor stole money from the church offering plates. As far as the missing peridot is concerned, unfortunately, I've yet to make any headway.

A witch's coven in Salida gifted the large, dazzling jewel to the town in 1885. They gave it to the town founder to thank him for saving their High Priestess when her boot got caught in the railroad tracks. With a train barreling down on her, Mr. Cooper risked his life to free her from certain death.

The witches told them that keeping the peridot on the enchanted pedestal in the museum would ensure good fortune and health for all. Then they cast a spell over it to keep it safe. Anyone attempting to steal the peridot would be cursed forever.

For well over 100 years, Glenwood Springs' residents, along with tourists from all over the world, have visited the stone, hoping its magic would rub off on them.

It's the world's second-largest peridot at 304 carats. I saw it in the museum when I first moved here. It's an awe-inspiring, brilliant green, sparkling gemstone. But not dark green like an emerald. It's more of a deep golden green, like the color of grass in June.

I was shocked to see it resting on a plush, red velvet pedestal with no cover or locks to keep it safe. They assured me that it was carefully guarded by the original coven's spell.

When I pointed out that, obviously, it wasn't guarded *that* carefully, they responded with horrified gasps. Yes, sometimes I still say the most inappropriate things out loud.

Secretly, I don't think I believe in the idea of a gem that brings good fortune, but many of the town's residents, including the mayor, do. Now that it's missing, they believe the city is in peril.

Although as Juliet pointed out recently, I talk to ghosts, including my talking-ghost-cat-roommate, so perhaps anything is possible? Maybe I shouldn't dismiss the idea of a protective gem. Especially here in Glenwood Springs.

The mayor is extra nervous with the new year only a week away. She's begging me to find it before the clock strikes midnight on December 31. She insists we can't start the new year with misfortune hanging over our heads. However, without leads I don't see how it's possible.

The three ghosts who live in the museum have been no help whatsoever. When it was stolen, they were watching reruns of *Bewitched* on the little tv the security guard keeps in his office. What was the security guard doing at the time? Sleeping in front of the tv.

So far, no one has tried to sell it on the black market. Ronald Thurman, Glenwood's infamous retired jewel thief, who gave up a life of crime to consult with the FBI, is keeping a careful eye on those, but no luck.

Fast forward to Christmas Day, where the entire town has gathered in the Grand Ballroom at the Red Castle Hotel for the annual Christmas party. I know, who goes to a party on Christmas Day in real life, right? I was skeptical at first, too. But it's a thing here.

I've never seen the ballroom this festive. Thousands of colorful twinkling lights surround it. Fat red candles rest in the middle of tables while shadows from the bright flames dance across glittering white tablecloths. Fresh evergreen boughs and thick bushy Christmas trees add a delightful pine scent to the festivities.

The liquor is flowing. The food is decadent. Name any cocktail or liqueur, the wait staff has it covered. Wendy obviously favors peppermint martinis, although I suspect they won't seem as delightful in the morning.

I'm sticking to champagne. Yes, the authentic French stuff. Juliet prefers hard apple cider from one of the local breweries. She tells me the Sour Cherry flavor from a brewery on Colorado's Western Slope is the best.

As for the food, where do I start? There's something here for everyone. Gluten-free, vegan, low-calorie, high-calorie, and keto are just the options I can remember off the top of my head.

There's the most delectable prime rib roast I've ever laid eyes on, charcuterie boards with an endless variety of cheeses, meats, nuts, and fruit, pasta dishes galore, along with a vat of mashed potatoes and gravy that's big enough to swim in.

The desserts? Don't get me started on the desserts. An array of tantalizing pies, cakes, cookies, and candies that would take me a lifetime to try one of each.

Still, the party is subdued. The misfortune the town has experienced recently weighs on everyone's minds. Many shopkeepers report that business is way down. They fear they'll go bankrupt soon if things don't turn around.

There was an unexpected blizzard in September, which has never happened here. Enormous tree branches weighed down under heavy wet snow snapped like twigs.

During the storm, the town's largest and oldest evergreen tree fell on top of a power line. Nearly a third of the city was without power for two weeks. Then a rare strain of bird flu struck, affecting hundreds of people.

School was canceled for almost a month, shops were closed, and the hospital was severely short-staffed. I still say it's a coincidence, but many are nervous and planning to move away if the peridot isn't found soon.

The city council even considered canceling the party for the first time since World War II out of fear that something dreadful would happen. Still, they ultimately decided it could bolster everyone's spirits and may be just what everyone needed. Besides, it's Christmas. What could possibly go wrong?

2

I've had mixed feelings about the holidays for a long time. Christmas with my parents was always the greatest day ever. Mom would get up early to make her special French toast. I'd give anything now to replicate it. I've tried repeatedly but can't get it quite right. Christmas with my husband Ben was fabulous too. Our first Christmas together was the first I had with a real family since my parents died.

But after he was killed in Afghanistan serving with the Army Rangers, I quit celebrating altogether. I'd like to tell you I volunteered at the homeless veterans' shelter, passing out hot meals and cheer, but I didn't. I sat at home in the dark, feeling sorry for myself.

Then Christmas as a foster kid was always bleak. But I understand it now. Foster families had multiple kids. They couldn't be expected to hand out gifts like bikes and video games. We got the obligatory socks and lip balm. The socks were always appreciated, though.

Out of habit, I didn't plan to do anything special at home this year. But Clara, my 143-year-old roommate, who is eternally destined to wear the pink flannel nightgown she died in, begged me for a Christmas tree. At first, I did it just to make her happy. But once it was decorated and lit, even I had to admit it felt good to have a pretty tree again.

While a traditional ghost is confined to the property where they passed, for some reason, Clara and Mystery the cat can ride along in the obnoxiously pink refurbished Volkswagen Bus that the previous homeowners left behind because they thought it was haunted. Turns out they were right, thanks to Clara.

So, Clara insisted we pick out a Christmas tree together. You can imagine the salesman's face when I kept turning back to argue with what appeared to be an empty bus, with Clara shouting instructions on picking the perfect tree the entire time. No doubt he was relieved when we were done.

While decorating the tree, Clara was just as picky, instructing me on how best to arrange the ornaments, lights, and tinsel. Mystery regaled us with tales of the number of

Christmas trees she knocked over in her day. Oddly, what started as a way to appease Clara turned out to be a really fun day. It felt like family for the first time in forever.

I was speechless when I came downstairs this morning to find the tree fully lit, Clara and Mystery waiting for me. Clara felt bad that she couldn't make French toast, but I assured her that waking up to find my special roommates waiting for me was enough.

Then Wendy and Juliet surprised all of us with coffee and fresh bagels from Juliet's bakery. We even exchanged gifts. For Juliet, a newly published book of spells and some handmade, decorated hair clips made from a shop in town, for her long blonde hair.

For Wendy, new earrings for each one of her piercings and a gift certificate for a massage. As for me, I was rather embarrassed as I stared down at the brightly wrapped present bearing a bright red, crisp bow. I bit my lip to keep from blubbering. Wendy explained it was just a little something. No need to cry. It's not like it was a new car.

I told her it was more than just a little something. It was the first Christmas gift I'd gotten in a very long time. One of the few since my parents died. To me, it wasn't little. It was the world.

It was a set of enchanted specialty teas and candles made by Wendy. Teas to help ease a variety of issues, such as anxiety, impatience, and promoting relaxation. She knows me well! When I first met her, she gave me a tea that helped me make an important decision that ultimately changed all our lives.

When Juliet handed me her present, the happy tears began again. It was a cookbook with recipes submitted by moms. It was incredibly thoughtful.

It's the best Christmas I've had in many years. Clara said it was for her, too, considering she usually just watches the family who lives here, in silence. This year she got to join in and celebrate. I still haven't volunteered at the veterans' homeless shelter, but I sent them a big check. I may not be passing out food, but at least my donation helped them buy it. The entire day has been one delightful surprise after another.

I'll never forget it. I gaze at Wendy and Juliet across the table, my heart overflowing with gratitude. Aside from Ben, they're the first real friends I've ever had.

Yet sadness washes over me for just a moment. Ben would have loved Glenwood. He always made friends easier than I did. He didn't go through life with a big chip on his shoulder like me.

I like to think, however, that life in Glenwood Springs has shrunk that chip considerably. I never told Ben I talk to ghosts. I always planned to. Then he was gone, and it was too late. He was the love of my life. I'm convinced that kind of love only comes around once *if* a person is lucky. I just wish I'd been more honest with him.

While nibbling on my third ginger snap, Juliet and I discuss plans for New Year's Eve. We're interrupted when a hush falls over the ballroom. Somewhere across the way, a dropped fork clatters loudly against a glass plate. At the table next to us, Mr. Barley, who has obviously had too much to drink as well, continues talking loudly. His wife quickly shushes him.

All eyes turn to the doorway where a sizeable blonde man stands. He surveys the room, folding his arms across his broad chest, looking formidable.

3

That sizeable blonde man is Gabriel Molina, the new manager of the Red Castle Hotel, which makes him my boss. He gets that stunned reaction a lot. Ever since he got to town, rumors have circulated fast and furious that he's what we call a shifter.

Most are convinced he transforms into a large yellow dog. At 6'4", I'm guessing that's one big dog. If the rumors are true, that is. Party guests continue to stare while he approaches our table.

I gulp when he places a large paw, I mean hand, on my shoulder. When he kneels to get closer to me. My cheeks flush while everyone stares. "I'm sorry to bother you during the party, Holly, but do you think you could come in to work an hour early tomorrow?" he asks quietly.

When I first moved to Glenwood, I had just been unceremoniously fired from my job as a cybersecurity consultant. I saw a help-wanted flyer at the gas station seeking a bartender at the Red Castle Hotel. I was sure that working as a bartender would be far less stressful than my previous job.

While waiting for my interview, Mr. Sinclair, the manager at the time, caught me talking to a ghost. He begged me to work as a spirit communicator instead. They needed someone who could converse with the hotel ghosts to help solve the mystery of a missing tiara.

I reluctantly agreed as long as I could work as a bartender like I originally planned. Solving that mystery led to my becoming a Paranormal Private Investigator.

Yet I still help at the hotel bar from time to time. They're especially busy now with Christmas parties and tourists, so I've been helping a lot lately.

"Sure, no problem." I nod, swigging my champagne.

"Thank you so much." He gives me a toothy grin.

"Gabriel, won't you join us for a Christmas cocktail?" Juliet suggests.

"Yes! Join us!" Wendy exclaims, awkwardly patting the empty chair next to her. When she slurs her words, Juliet slides the half-drunk peppermint martini away.

"Wendy has been over-served this evening," she says. "Excuse me, waiter. Can we get a large glass of water for her and..." She points at Gabriel questioningly.

"Irish neat, water back, please," he tells the waiter, who nods sharply, hurrying away to fill the order.

"Wow, you even drink like a man." Wendy giggles. "So, tell me. Are the rumors true? Are you really a--"

"--annnd we're done here!" Juliet exclaims, stuffing a bacon-wrapped water chestnut into Wendy's mouth before she finishes her question.

Wendy looks annoyed at first but then smiles as she chews on the tantalizing morsel. "Man, those are good! Have you had any of these?" she asks, pushing the tray in Gabriel's direction.

"Did you have a good Christmas?" he asks me, holding his hand up to decline the appetizer.

Wendy shrugs, popping another one into her mouth, chewing loudly while Juliet rolls her eyes.

"One of the best ever!" I exclaim.

"Well, that's nice to hear."

"How about you?" I ask him.

"Mine was low key. I slept in, then I called my mom, then I came here to catch up on some paperwork and get ready for the big party. Nothing too exciting. Not like yours, apparently," he laughs.

"If I'd known you didn't have anything to do, I would have invited you over!" I tell him.

"Yes, I must meet your trouble-making roommates someday," he says. "Even though I wouldn't be able to see them, of course."

"I'm good at translating," I assure him. Six months ago, I was terrified someone would learn of my secret. Now everyone knows I see dead people. The best part is no one really seems to care. I get far more attention from driving around in the bright pink bus than I do from talking to ghosts.

We discuss the drink menu that the accountants requested for their small Boxing Day party in the conference room tomorrow. We also go over how to handle the New Year's Eve party that the Capping Crowns, the dentists' professional union, is hosting at the hotel and how we can ward off any potential trouble there, as they're often a rowdy bunch. I know, whoda thunk?

Our conversation consists mainly of small talk and work issues, but from time to time, I notice Juliet and Wendy with their heads together giggling. I give them the best salty look I have to shut them up, but it doesn't help.

"See you tomorrow, Holly," Gabriel tells me as he gets up to leave.

"See you," I tell him.

After he leaves, Wendy giggles while Juliet tries to silence her.

"What?" I ask.

"He likes you!" Wendy says in a singsong voice.

"Oh please," I groan. "He's my boss."

"He's not the only one who likes you," Juliet says, pointing her head toward Sheriff Mack, who quickly looks away when he sees us watching him.

"She's like the town's most eligible bachelorette." Wendy giggles again.

"You're drunk." I jab my finger at Wendy, "You're just out of your mind," I tell Juliet.

"Puhhhhleeeeze," Juliet moans. "The entire time Gabriel was here, Sheriff Mack glared at him."

I roll my eyes. "You're just bored. You're inventing drama that isn't there."

"Whatever you say," Juliet says, peering over the tops of her turquoise cat glasses while sipping her cider.

4

Thankfully, Wendy interrupts with a caterwauling wail that must have alerted dogs from as far away as Grand Junction. "Dashing through the snow..." she sings loudly. Although *sings* is pushing it. She taps the glasses in front of her with a fork, convinced she's playing a tune.

"Seriously, that's it," Juliet proclaims when one breaks. "We need to get some non-alcoholic fluids in her," she begs me, while motioning a waiter to help clean up.

"I'm on it. Why don't I get everyone some coffee," I suggest, gesturing to the coffee station in the corner.

"Good idea!" Juliet nods.

When I get there, I find the hospital chaplain pouring a cup.

"Merry Christmas, chaplain!" I greet him.

"Well, Merry Christmas to you, Holly!" he responds brightly. "Are you having a good time?"

"You know what? I am!" I exclaim.

"You sound surprised," he chuckles.

"Actually, I am surprised!" We both laugh at how silly that sounds. "It's been the best Christmas I've had in many years."

"Glad to hear it!" he beams.

"How about you? How has your Christmas been?" I ask.

"Marvelous! Tomorrow the children's choir is singing at the nursing home. The residents will be so excited!"

"Do you know someone in the nursing home?" I inquire.

"I'm the chaplain." Upon seeing my confusion, he explains. "The hospital *and* the nursing home share me."

"Oh! I didn't realize that."

"Good evening, Chaplain, Ms. Daniel," Sheriff Mack says, joining us at the coffee station.

"Merry Christmas, Sheriff!" the chaplain exclaims. "Thank you again for your generous toy donation for the hospitalized children."

When I lift my eyebrow quizzically, I swear the sheriff blushes just a bit.

"Every year, the Sheriff's Department collects toys for children in the hospital," the chaplain tells me.

"It's not that big of a deal," Sheriff Mack grunts.

"Not that big of a deal?" he squeaks. "Under Sheriff Mack's leadership, the toys the department collects have tripled! In years past, we often didn't have enough toys to go around. We had to invent clever ways to ensure each child got something."

I inwardly cringe, remembering my present-less years in the foster system.

"With Sheriff Mack at the helm, his people collect so many gifts that this year we had plenty for children in the hospital *and* kids at the orphanage," he proclaims, grinning at Sheriff Mack.

"Well done, Steve," I tell him in a rare moment of camaraderie.

He shrugs while getting very busy putting cream in his coffee, but I can tell he's secretly pleased with the attention. I didn't know he did this. Next year I'll donate to the veterans' homeless shelter *and* the toy drive.

"Yoo hoo! Chaplain!" a table of elderly ladies call out as he waves back.

"If you'll excuse me, folks, my mahjong club awaits," he tells us, scurrying to join his friends, leaving us alone.

"I see *you're* enjoying the party," Sheriff Mack says with a hint of irony.

"I am," I tell him. "I admit it seemed a little ridiculous at first, the thought of a town party on Christmas Day, but it's been really fun."

"As paranoid as everyone is, since that shiny rock went missing, I wasn't sure the party was such a great idea, but so far, so good."

The corners of my mouth turn up just a tad when he refers to the Precious Peridot as a shiny rock. "Not a believer, huh?" I ask.

"Not really." He shakes his head. "You?"

"Not really," I agree. Wow, we're just agreeing all over the place tonight. But when he wanders off without another word, I realize our conversation is over. What an odd duck that one is.

Somehow, I carry three cups of coffee, albeit precariously, back to our table without spilling a drop. Once I settle in my seat again, Juliet and I chat about how good the food was tonight.

While we sip our coffee, a disheveled Gabriel strides determinedly across the ballroom.

"Where did he come from?" Juliet asks.

"I think he came through the employee entrance," I tell her.

I assume from the pink cheeks he was outside in the cold. But where did he get those scratches on his face?

"His face wasn't scratched before, was it?" I ask, concerned.

"I don't think so," Juliet responds, shaking her head slowly.

"It wasn't!" Wendy declares. "I should know. I was staring at him."

When I look again, I notice his unkempt hair and dirt smudged on his shirt, which I'm sure wasn't there before, either. What the heck was he doing outside? Wrestling? We're not the only ones who notice the change. The entire ballroom gawks at him as he hurries to the doorway leading to his office.

"I bet he was outside shifting into a dog!" Wendy exclaims in an abnormally loud stage whisper.

"You just keep drinking that coffee, sweetie," Juliet urges.

"Maybe he was running through the woods!" Wendy continues.

When several people at nearby tables turn to stare at us, Juliet buries her head in her hands.

"Hey, I should go outside too!" Wendy declares.

"That's a good idea. I think we could all use some fresh air," Juliet says.

Juliet and I make our way to the main door when we realize Wendy isn't with us. She's moving toward the back where Gabriel just came from.

"Why is she going out the employee exit?" I ask.

"Who knows, but we better follow her," Juliet insists.

We quicken our pace to catch up to Wendy, who's singing again. She wanders down the hallway and out the door, mangling the words to I Want a Hippopotamus for Christmas. Whoever wrote that song should be banished to another planet. It never fails. Every year I hear it once on the radio then it's stuck in my head the entire season.

"Brrr! We should have brought our coats!" Juliet exclaims, rubbing her arms when we hit the frigid night air.

"Here comes Santa Claus!" Wendy sings. "Hey, your guys, it's so cold I can see my breath!"

"She'll feel that in the morning," I tell Juliet, shaking my head.

Juliet and I keep close to the door as Wendy wanders over to the dumpster area, singing Happy Birthday. Who knew she was a singing drunk? Better than an angry drunk, I suppose.

"Can't we go back inside?" I ask. "I'm freezing."

"We can't go without her," Juliet insists, jabbing her thumb in Wendy's direction. "She'll fall and freeze to death."

"Fine. One more minute," I tell her. "Then I'm going inside."

We pause while blowing into our hands to keep warm. It doesn't work.

"Hey, ladies!" Wendy shouts. "Someone is asleep back here!"

"Oh dear, what is she talking about now?" Juliet ponders.

"I hate to think," I mutter while we shuffle in Wendy's direction. I swear it's too cold to even walk properly.

My jaw drops in shock after we circle around the short brick wall that hides the dumpsters from the rest of the world.

"Oh no!" Juliet cries out.

The chaplain is slumped against the dumpster. He's most definitely not asleep.

5

"**C**haplain Palmer!" I wail, kneeling to check for a pulse—my hand trembling as I reach for his neck. The light isn't great out here, but I swear he has finger-shaped bruising around his throat. I most definitely didn't see that before.

"What do you think you're doing?" Sheriff Mack bellows just as my fingers touch the chaplain.

"Yeep!" Wendy shrieks, jumping behind the dumpster to hide.

"Sheriff, we just discovered him like this. You have to help!" Juliet begs.

"Back away, Holly!" he demands.

I back up, muttering, "There's no pulse."

With an unobstructed view of the chaplain, the sheriff curses. He, too, bends down to check for a pulse while calling on his phone for backup and the Medical Examiner's office. After confirming there's no pulse, he pivots to glare at me. My memory flashes back to when he discovered me with Mr. Beasley's body only a few months ago at the doll museum.

I wrack my brain for a quip or excuse, but unable to find one, I shrug instead. He glares harder. Oops. That seemed cavalier. I don't know what else to do, though. He can't think *we* had anything to do with this.

"You three, follow me. Don't touch anything!" he growls.

After directing us away from the crime scene, he pulls a small blue notepad from his suit pocket. Does he carry that everywhere he goes? "Let's start from the top, ladies. What happened here?" When all of us talk at once, he groans loudly, pinching the bridge of his nose. "One at a time," he sighs.

I turn to Juliet. "You start."

The story of how we followed Wendy outside because we didn't want her to be alone pours out of her. She ends with Wendy wandering over to the dumpsters only to discover the chaplain's body.

"So, you lost sight of Wendy for a time?" he confirms.

"Yes, but there's no way she did this!" I fling my hand toward the body.

Sirens pierce the bitter night air, growing closer by the second, forcing us to pause for a moment.

"Then why did she hide when she saw me?" he asks.

"She's drunk. She was just goofing around," I assure him.

"How long exactly did you lose sight of her?"

"We told you it was just a moment," Juliet reminds him.

"How long is a moment for you? Three seconds? Five minutes?" he presses impatiently.

Juliet stares at me pleadingly.

"Whatever it was, it wasn't long enough for her to strangle a man his size. He's not exactly small, you know!" I counter.

"How do you know he was strangled?" he asks.

"I saw odd finger-shaped bruises on his neck that I know weren't there before when we talked to him at the coffee station," I insist.

"Ohhh, I forgot, you're a private investigator!" He mocks me.

"That's Paranormal Private Investigator to you!" Wendy slurs.

Gee, thanks for the help, Wendy.

Sheriff Mack rolls his eyes. He doesn't like that I investigate mysteries. *Leave it up to the trained professionals* he frequently lectures.

But as a Paranormal Private Investigator and spirit communicator, even he has to admit I can do things he can't.

Juliet and I cringe when two patrol cars screech to a halt next to us; their blue and red lights illuminate the night sky while casting an eerie glow across the landscape.

"Don't move!" he jabs his finger at us before marching over to the cars to confer with his deputies.

"The lights are so pretty," Wendy whispers.

"Oh, sober up already!" Juliet snaps.

Whoa. Usually, I'm the one losing my temper and snapping at people. Juliet is the even-keeled, mature mother figure among us.

"What happens next?" Wendy asks.

"Don't you have a spell to sober her up?" I ask Juliet.

"I would give her a sobriety serum if I had one on me," she responds.

"I hope you at least have something for a nasty hangover," I point out.

"I do," she says, nodding her head.

"Let me guess, that's at home too."

"It sure is," she admits.

"Who do you think could have done this?" I ask.

"I didn't get a clear look at him; I was so freaked out. Did he really look like he was strangled?"

I nod my head reluctantly. "It was pretty gruesome."

"That's awful." Juliet shudders.

"Do you know if he had any enemies?" I ask her.

"Not that I know of!" she exclaims. "Everybody loved him. He collected Christmas toys for children in the hospital. He played mah jong with little old ladies. How could a man like that have enemies?" she asks.

"Heyyyy," Wendy drawls. "Is his ghost here?"

"No, his ghost isn't here," I inform her.

"Because that would be super handy, wouldn't it? Then you could just ask him who killed him, amiright?"

Wendy may be drunk, but she's right. It would certainly be a lot easier if his ghost were hanging around. I thought the same thing when I found Mr. Beasley's body. But nothing is ever that easy, is it?

Sheriff Mack returns with a deputy in tow. Of course, it has to be Deputy Owens, who I encountered last summer after Mr. Beasley was murdered. Even though we helped each other at the end of the investigation, we aren't exactly friends.

"Deputy Owens will take your statements," Sheriff Mack explains.

"Let's go inside where it's warmer, ladies." His eyes narrow when he recognizes me.

This should be fun. My mind is awhirl while we file in through the same door we just exited. How could this happen? On Christmas of all days? Who would do such a thing? It seems like I just saw him at the coffee station a few minutes ago.

When I look at the clock, though, I'm surprised to realize it was an hour ago. The last person I saw him with was me. And the sheriff. No, wait, I watched him walk over to the table to play mah jong. I seriously doubt any of them are capable of strangling a man.

And the last person I saw come through the employee entrance was - gulp - Gabriel.

6

"Is this your office?" Deputy Owens asks the head chef.

"It is," he answers.

"I need it to question these women. Official business on behalf of the Sheriff's Department."

"Sure, help yourself." He shrugs.

"You wait out here," Deputy Owens points at Juliet and me. "You," he gestures at Wendy, "come with me."

Wendy dutifully follows him into the office while he shuts the door in our faces.

"I hope she doesn't break into song while she's in there," Juliet says.

"I kind of hope she does," I admit.

"Okay, I do, too," she laughs.

Several minutes later, Wendy exits the office with the deputy looking irritable.

"You're next." He points at Juliet.

"Good luck!" I tell her.

"How did it go?" I ask Wendy.

"He's so nice," Wendy tells me. "He wanted to know all about how my night went." I told him about those delicious peppermint martinis and all our scrumptious food. He also said he'd come by the bookstore first thing in the morning to talk to me again!"

"I'm sure he did." No doubt hoping she'll be sober by then.

The minutes tick by while we wait for Juliet to finish. I grab two bottles of water out of the refrigerator. "Here," I tell Wendy. "Drink this. You'll thank me later."

Wendy guzzles the water without singing, which is good. I think she's sobering up.

Just as I'm about to knock on the door to ensure everything is all right, Juliet and Deputy Owens emerge from the office. He crooks his finger at me. I step into the office while he clicks the door shut behind me.

"Have a seat, Ms. Daniel," he orders, pointing to a chair against the wall. "Start from the beginning. I need your version of what happened when you and your friends exited the building tonight. Specifically, why you chose to go out the back door, the employee entrance, rather than the front."

"As you've undoubtedly noticed, Wendy had a lot to drink tonight," I point out.

"I did notice." He nods.

"Juliet and I were trying to get her to drink anything other than another peppermint martini. We gave her water and coffee. Then she said she wanted to go outside, so we thought some fresh air would help."

"That still doesn't answer why you went out the back door," he grumbles.

"Well, uh," I hesitate when I remember it was Wendy who chose the back door.

"Go on," he prods.

"We just decided to go out the back."

"Mmm hmm."

I don't know why he thinks our door choice is important. If the chaplain was strangled, there's no way Wendy did it that fast. I should never have admitted to them in the first place that she found the chaplain's body. It's not important, anyway.

"You told the sheriff that you and Juliet were waiting by the back door when Wendy entered the dumpster area."

"That's right," I tell him.

"Could you see what she was doing back there?"

"No, but we could hear her singing."

"What was she singing?" he asks.

"I think she was singing Happy Birthday right before she found the chaplain."

"Did you see anyone else in the area?" his pen hesitates over his notebook while he glares at me.

"Nope!" I shake my head.

"Did you *hear* anything else?"

"Again, no," I insist.

"Did you see anyone else enter or exit the employee door tonight before you and your friends used it?"

I hesitate. I didn't actually see Gabriel near the door. I was sure he'd been outside, and he came from the *direction* of the door, but I'm not lying when I say I didn't see him near the door.

"Why the hesitation?" he asks.

"Errr, I'm just thinking. I want to get this right. We have a killer to find, after all."

"Did you or did you not see anyone else use the employee door shortly before you used it this evening?"

"I did not see anyone else using that door shortly before we used it," I respond, choosing my words carefully.

He tilts his head at me. "How well do you know the chaplain?" he asks.

"Not that well. I know who he is, and he knows, uh, knew who I was. I mean, we knew each other by name. I can tell you he works at the hospital. Oh, and I just found out he works at the nursing home. But that's about it."

"Did you touch anything? Move anything while you were back there? Did you dispose of anything? A potential clue, perhaps?"

"Of course not!" I retort.

"Sheriff Mack told me he found you kneeling over the body with your hand against his neck."

"I was hoping he might still be alive!" I exclaim.

"I asked if you touched anything, and you emphatically said no. So I'll ask you again. Did you touch anything when you were with the body?"

"Other than touching his neck to check for a pulse, no, I didn't touch anything when I was with the body."

"Okay, well, that's all the questions I have for you this evening. Please make yourself available if our department needs to question you further."

"Of course," I tell him. I thought Sheriff Mack was annoying. This guy is way worse.

7

I breathe an audible sigh of relief when Deputy Owens opens the door to free me. Juliet understands when I roll my eyes at her, silently indicating that everything is fine, but that the deputy hasn't become any less annoying in the last several minutes.

"Uhh, I don't feel so great," Wendy moans from the floor.

"Why is she on the floor?"

"She insisted the chair she was sitting on was spinning," Juliet explains, shaking her head.

I cringe when I spy the chef glaring at Wendy for having the audacity to lie on his kitchen floor. He runs a tight ship back here, and we don't dare mess with him.

"Sorry, Jerry, we'll be out of your hair in a jiffy," I plead.

When he purses his lips at me, I know we only have a brief window before he really starts yelling.

"You'll need to exit through the ballroom," Deputy Owens explains. "The back is cordoned off."

"Blast it!" Juliet grimaces. "I was hoping to avoid that area."

"Maybe we'll get lucky, and everyone has gone home," I offer.

"When do we ever get that lucky?" Wendy mumbles from the floor.

Good point.

"Up and atem," Juliet says, offering Wendy her hand. "Don't worry," she assures me, patting my shoulder when she notices my look of concern for a wobbling Wendy. "I have an anti-toxin potion she can drink. She'll be right as rain."

"How many of those martinis did she have?" I ask.

"Too many!" Wendy bellows.

"At least she quit singing," Juliet points out.

"Yes, there's that," I agree.

I crack open the door, peering into the ballroom, hoping against hope that it's cleared out. Ugh. Wendy was right. We're never that lucky. Several groups huddle together, speaking in hushed tones. No doubt gossiping about the police activity behind the hotel. I glance longingly at the back door.

"Don't even think about it," Deputy Owens growls.

Drat. "Here goes nothing," I tell the ladies.

The moment we enter the ballroom, curious guests swarm us, firing a barrage of questions at us about the police activity. Juliet and I answer everyone's questions to the best of our ability. We don't really know much. Yes, we found the chaplain's body by the dumpsters. No, Wendy didn't kill him. No, we don't know for certain how he died.

The questions go on and on. Some are downright ludicrous. I wonder how these stories start. No, the chaplain wasn't killed by a famous mobster in a drive-by shooting. At least, I don't think so.

No, the chaplain wasn't killed by a grizzly bear while defending a one-armed orphan. Pretty sure there'd be scratches and blood. Besides, where's the orphan? Inevitably, someone mentions Gabriel.

"Hey, didn't you see the shifter cut through here right before they went outside?" a man mentions.

"Yeah! I did!" some woman exclaims.

"Hey, me too!" someone across the room chimes in.

Uh oh. This isn't good. To be certain, if for some reason, Gabriel killed the chaplain; then they should lock him up and throw away the key. But I still can't imagine him killing anybody. I also hate the thought of people judging him unfairly because they think he transforms into a dog or whatever.

First, we don't know for sure that he's a shifter. Second, even if he is, that doesn't automatically make him a killer. I know little about shifters, but they're pretty much like any other paranormal being. Except for maybe vampires and werewolves, but I don't know if I've ever met one of those, either.

"Listen up, everybody!" Deputy Owens announces. "We've had an incident on the premises this evening. We need to interview each of you before you leave tonight!" The partiers groan in protest.

"Don't be like that!" he pleads. "There's still plenty to eat. Grab yourselves another dessert and a coffee. We'll have this wrapped up in a wink."

The party guests perk up at the thought of an extra dessert. I doubt that any of them saw anything, anyway. At this point, it's probably a lot of gossip and innuendo.

"You three are obviously free to go." He points at us. We collect our things while Juliet messages for a cab. Considering the whole town turned out tonight, the rides are free. They didn't want to take a chance on any accidents. City Council decided with all the recent bad luck, they shouldn't tempt fate. Although who had "strangled holy man" on *their* bingo card? I sure didn't!

8

— ◦ —

"You're sure she isn't dead?" Mystery asks.

"I don't think so!" Clara says.

"What was that racket she was making last night? Because it sure sounded to me like she was dying!"

"It's called snoring," Clara explains. "My dear Marvin snored like a freight train. It was awful."

"I don't snore!" I insist. "And I'm not dead," I grumble opening my eyes just a crack to find my roommates with their ghostly faces floating inches from mine.

"The TV news said you found another body," Mystery informs me.

That's right. I don't just live with a talking ghost cat. I live with a talking ghost cat who watches tv. Then my other ghostly roommate doesn't just watch tv. She also reads the newspaper.

"I didn't find the body; Wendy did," I tell them. The sunlight streaming through the window hurts my eyes. "What time is it?"

"It's 8:00," Clara tells me.

"Seriously?" I exclaim. I never sleep this late. I guess I'm not swimming laps this morning. I hope Wendy and Juliet got home all right. Part of me wants to roll over and go back to sleep.

"The tv said Gabriel Molina is a suspect in the chaplain's murder. Isn't that your boss at the hotel?" Clara asks.

"What?" I shriek, bolting upright in bed.

"Didn't you tell me people think he's a shifter?" Clara asks.

"Yes, but back up for a second."

Clara actually backs up, and I have to try not to laugh.

"Did you say the shif--, I mean Gabriel is a suspect?" I ask.

"I didn't say it; the tv said it. I'm just repeating it."

"Okay, fine, whatever." I can't believe they're already calling him a suspect.

"They interviewed a bunch of people who said they saw him looking all scratched up and dirty right before they found the body."

I'm struggling to process all this, but my brain is still foggy from sleeping so soundly. "Where are my slippers?" I ask, swinging my legs off the bed.

"They're right where you always keep them," Mystery says, tilting her head toward them.

While I slide my feet into my fuzzy bunny slippers, my mind churns with the possibility that Gabriel is the killer. I still can't believe that he could do something like that. I don't know him that well, but he never struck me as the violent type. "Have they arrested him?" I ask.

"I don't think so," Clara says, shaking her head.

"I need coffee," I mutter, shuffling toward the stairs. I love this old house, right down to the creaky stairs. The fragrant, green Christmas tree sits in the large picture window overlooking the patio.

Remarkably well-preserved wood flooring leads into the spacious kitchen where I have yet to learn to cook. When I bought this big, beautiful house I couldn't believe what a good deal I got.

It was only after we closed that I learned it was haunted! I know in the beginning I said I was mad that it came with two spirit roommates, but that was months ago. Besides, what better house for a spirit communicator, right?

While the kitchen fills with the heavenly smell of brewing coffee, I step onto the patio to get the newspaper. We haven't used it much since the cold weather set in. But last summer we spent many evenings on the patio, drinking iced tea while enjoying the sounds of the nearby rushing Colorado River. It's much quieter now that it's partially frozen.

"Hey, you guys, it's snowing again!" I call out, watching snowflakes slowly drift down from the gray sky. Glenwood Springs is nestled in a mountain valley and everywhere I turn I see majestic peaks reaching for the clouds. If I thought this town was beautiful in the summer, it's nothing compared to its unique beauty when snow blankets the mountains in winter.

This morning while the town sleeps, there's a magical kind of peaceful presence. I pause for a moment to take it all in. When I first moved here, I was still angry about so many things that had happened to me in the past. Now I'm just grateful to live in this idyllic place surrounded by my dear friends.

"What are you doing on the patio gawking at the snow?" Clara shouts. "Get in here before you catch a cold."

So much for a quiet moment of gratitude.

"You do know you can't catch a cold from standing outside in the snow, right?" I ask Clara.

"Back in my day, you could!" she insists. She rushes over to check out the newspaper after I spread it out on the kitchen table. She's the main reason I get a newspaper. Even though she watches the news on TV, she still likes to read the Glenwood Gazette.

She tells me she has fond memories of her dad sitting at the kitchen table with his breakfast, reading the paper before going to work in the Mt. Harris coal mines. As soon as he finished, she and her sisters would fight over who got to read the funny pages first.

This morning's news sure is a lot of doom and gloom for the day after Christmas. The front page has the news of Chaplain Palmer's murder. There's a picture of the Red Castle Hotel with the sheriff's cars parked in front. Party guests huddle together, looking distraught.

"At least it isn't an awful picture of me this time, right?" I tell Clara. When I was a suspect in Mr. Beasley's arrest last summer, the paper printed the worst picture of me possible. Juliet said I looked like death eating a cracker. Gee thanks. I mean, it was awful, but I didn't need confirmation with such colorful terms.

Then, just as I think I'm off the hook, Clara points to a picture on the next page. It's a beaut—a picture of Juliet, Wendy, and me coming out of the hotel. Only Wendy is leaning over a planter, looking like she's about to barf. Or perhaps she was already mid-barf at that point.

My eyes scan a hit piece written by some know it all reporter. She insinuates that the killer must be Gabriel Molina because, one: he's new in town, and two: he's probably a shifter and, therefore, not only untrustworthy but violent as well. She also claims he's part of the misfortune brought on by the missing peridot. What a vile woman.

"Now the question is, what are you going to do about this?" Clara asks as I sip my coffee.

"Huh? What am I going to do about what?" I ask, taking another sip, hoping that will make things clearer.

"Solving the mystery, silly."

"Did someone call me?" Mystery laughs, marching through the kitchen.

Clara rolls her eyes. "The mystery of who killed Chaplain Palmer."

"Why are you looking at me?" I jab at myself with my finger, looking aghast. "Remember, I still need to find the Precious Peridot!"

"I'd say this takes precedence," she responds.

"I'd say you're out of your mind. Besides, Sheriff Mack would be furious if I get involved in this one, too."

"So, when has that ever stopped you?"

She has a point there. But still. I'm not taking this on. The mayor was nagging me again last night to find the Precious Peridot. The last thing I need to do is get involved in another murder mystery.

9

"**G**ood morning, everyone!" I call out, carefully knocking the snow from my boots first so I don't track it into the Looking Glass Bookstore.

"Shhh!" Wendy says grumpily. Oversized sunglasses block at least a third of her usually cheerful face.

"Sorry!" I whisper. "I thought you had an anti-hangover serum," I tell Juliet.

"You're looking at it," she says, pointing to an ugly green concoction Wendy is attempting to drink.

"This is horrible," she gags.

"Want some?" Juliet offers, holding up the blender carafe.

"No thanks, I'm good."

"I can't believe Chaplain Palmer is dead!" Wendy shudders.

"I can't believe you remember that," Juliet says.

"Finding a body isn't something you forget, no matter how many peppermint martinis you've had."

"You *thought* he was sleeping at first," I remind her.

"Okay, *that* part I forgot."

"Did you hear? That shifter from the hotel murdered the chaplain. On Christmas of all days. I knew we couldn't trust him," an elderly lady clucks to her friend in the corner of the bookstore.

"This is getting ugly." Juliet shakes her head sadly.

"They shouldn't judge *anyone* until all the facts are in," I respond angrily.

"Are you going to help solve the murder?" Wendy asks.

"Did Clara put you up to this?"

"Uhh, no, I can't talk to ghosts, remember?"

"She was pestering me to do the same thing!" I exclaim. "And the answer is no. I still have to find the peridot, in case you've forgotten. I trust Sheriff Mack and his department to do their jobs and catch the killer."

"If you say so." Wendy rolls her eyes.

"I do say so!"

"You guys! Come quick!" Tommy, a desk clerk from the Red Castle Hotel, shouts, bursting through the front door with such force we all jump.

"What's wrong now?" Juliet exclaims.

"Someone threw a brick through the window of the Red Castle Hotel!" he continues to shout.

"You're kidding me!" Juliet says.

"Come check it out for yourself!"

"Might as well see what he's talking about," I suggest.

"You ladies go. I'll stay here to drink my poison," Wendy says.

I glance at Juliet, who shrugs back. "Might as well check it out."

Juliet and I walk two blocks to the hotel, where a small crowd has gathered. I'm dismayed to see an ambulance parked at the curb with its lights flashing and the back doors open. "What the heck?" I mutter as we break into a slow jog.

"What's going on here?" Juliet asks.

A bystander points to the ambulance.

"Gabriel!" I cry out when I see the EMT checking out a nasty gash on his forehead. He's so tall that even sitting down, the paramedic has to stand on her toes to treat him.

"What happened?" Juliet asks, her voice cracking in distress.

"It's not a big deal, ladies." He waves his hands dismissively.

"Not a big deal?" I exclaim. "Your head is bleeding!"

"It's just a flesh wound!" he jokes, but winces when he tries to laugh.

"What happened?" I demand, when he doesn't answer Juliet.

"Someone threw a brick through my office window," he admits reluctantly.

"Why?"

He silently hands us a note written in crude black marker with block letters. YOU'LL PAY FOR WHAT YOU DID SHIFTER!

"Where did this come from?" I exclaim angrily, waving the note around.

"It was attached to the brick that came through the window."

"That's assault!" I shout. "Or attempted murder! Or something!"

"The police are on their way. I'm sure they'll take care of it."

How is he so calm? I'm disgusted and furious. I can't believe someone in our sleepy little mountain town is capable of this.

"How could this happen?" I turn to Juliet. By now, she knows me well enough to recognize my expression.

"Time to investigate?" she asks.

"You're darn right it is!" I exclaim.

10

If we were characters in a comic book, we'd have a dark cloud drawn over our heads as we trudge back to the bookstore. How discouraging!

"What is happening to this town?" Juliet laments.

"I don't know, but I'm making it my mission to find out," I tell her.

"What about the Precious Peridot?"

"Solving the chaplain's murder and exonerating Gabriel takes precedence," I respond somberly.

"What if they're connected?" she asks, wide-eyed.

"How would they be connected?" I scoff.

When she winces, I immediately regret saying it like that. Sometimes my temper still gets the best of me. I'm just really upset this is happening to Gabriel. I was bullied throughout my teen years for being different, but when I moved to Glenwood Springs, I was shocked, delightfully so, when I realized everyone here was so laid back.

To find out now that they're singling out someone for being different infuriates me. If we discover that Gabriel really did kill Chaplain Palmer, and I seriously doubt he did, then he'll face the appropriate consequences from the authorities. Not at the hands of a crazed mob.

Wendy is finishing up with a customer when we return to the store. "Tell me everything!" she demands after the customer gathers her purchases.

"The hangover cure seems to work!" I exclaim. The sunglasses are gone, and she's looking more alert. She's also styled her faux hawk since we last saw her. It's been adequately gelled and fluffed. Earlier it was sagging pitifully.

Wendy is horrified, of course, when we explain what happened. "You've decided to investigate, right?" When Juliet tries to suppress a smile, she shouts, "I knew it! I knew you couldn't stay away!"

"Now we need to figure out who killed the chaplain," I proclaim.

11

— • —

"Do you really think this will work?" Juliet asks as we head into the hospital.

"We have to start somewhere." I remind her, throwing my hands in the air. I don't even know what to look for while we're here or where we should start, but I'm certain at least one person here knows something about him.

Yikes. Who knew being a private investigator could be so frustrating? I don't know who stole the Precious Peridot, and I don't know who killed Chaplain Palmer. Maybe I should just stick to bartending instead.

"Can I help you?" a young woman at the check-in desk asks.

"Could you tell me where Chaplain Palmer's office is?"

She looks stricken. I should have been gentler when asking. "I, uh, er, uh, I don't know if--"

"It's okay." I put my hand up to stop her. "I know what happened."

"Oh, okay, good. I mean, good that I don't have to tell you," she says. "His office was on the third floor." At the word *was,* she chokes up a bit. Did this guy have a single enemy?

Just as Juliet presses the button marked 3 and the elevator doors start to close, a large hand grabs the elevator door, forcing it open.

The hand belongs to none other than Sheriff Mack. Uh oh. Do you think a *we're here to see a sick friend* story would work? He glares at us while assessing the situation. I can tell he's trying to think of a good reason to lecture us. When he reaches for the button marked 3, only to see it's already lit, that's his excuse.

"Let me guess. You're here to visit a sick friend," he says sarcastically. Juliet and I nod simultaneously while he pinches his lips together. "Mmm hmm."

When he pivots to face the elevator doors, I breathe a sigh of relief. Was it really that easy? Will we avoid a lengthy lecture on how we need to *leave it to the professionals?*

"Am I going to learn you're here investigating the chaplain's death?" he asks, shifting again to face us.

Drat. I should have known.

"I do possess certain skills that you don't, after all." I start. "I'm also a licensed private investigator," I throw in before he can respond.

"So you're here to talk to the ghosts?" he asks.

"I could be," I tell him, staring up at him with more nerve than I actually feel.

"How many ghosts have you talked to since you arrived?" he asks.

"As a matter of fact, I've seen four."

"Really. What did they say?"

"Unfortunately, they didn't say anything."

He rolls his eyes at me. It practically kills him that he must admit I see dead people. He doesn't want it to be true, but there have been too many occasions where the only way I could have known something was by talking to a ghost.

"There's a ghost in the elevator with us right now," I tell him.

He flinches just a teeny tiny bit. He wants to look around and ask where, but it's taking every ounce of self-control not to.

"Is there really a ghost in here?" Juliet whispers in my ear.

I nod. "Would you do me a favor and touch my friend's right shoulder?" I ask the elderly man in the corner.

"Sure." He shrugs. I'd tell him to do it to the sheriff, but I fear it would freak him out too much, and I'm not *that* mean. I know Juliet will get a kick out of it, however. The ghost touches her right shoulder, making her giggle.

"Oh, it's cold!" she says. "Do it again! Do it again!"

The ghost looks at her like she's a bit daft but obliges.

She shrieks. "That's so freaky!"

Sheriff Mack shakes his head in annoyance and turns around again to face the elevator doors. "Make sure you don't get in my way or hinder my investigation, or you'll earn yourself a quick trip to the station, got it?"

"You won't even know we're here, Sheriff!" Juliet insists.

"I doubt that," he mutters as the bell dings and the doors open.

From the looks of it, Sheriff Mack had already arranged to meet with someone in the chaplain's office. Juliet and I hang back, hoping to listen in on their conversation while appearing perfectly normal and not like we're creeping.

"Sheriff Mack, good to meet you, Peggy Sinclair, Human Resources Manager," she says, shaking his hand.

Human Resources, that's a good idea. She might know if he has any enemies at the hospital. Although, it's still hard to believe that he would. But then that stinker of a sheriff turns in our direction, smiles, goes into the chaplain's office, and shuts the door. Oh, that man!

"What do we do next?" Juliet asks.

"I dunno. Hang out and talk to people? See what they might know about Chaplain Palmer?"

"Works for me," she says.

"Psst!" a ghost in the corner beckons to me. His clothes and hair cut tell me he died in the 1950s or thereabout. If I had to guess, I'd say he was a truck driver. Maybe even a dockworker or warehouse employee. Each ghost I meet is its own little mystery.

"Hey there," I respond with a slight wave. "There's a ghost here," I tell Juliet.

"I gathered that," she laughs.

"What are you doing here?" he asks. "Is it true Chaplain Palmer was murdered last night?"

"Sadly, it is." I nod.

"Dat's too bad; he seemed like a nice fella. Kinda hard to be a chaplain at a hospital, I'd think. What wit all dem people dyin' and everything ya know?"

"Yeah, I know," I sigh. I remember when the Army chaplain and the Casualty Notification Officer knocked on my door to tell me Ben was killed in Iraq. It was 5:37 AM; the sun wasn't up yet. It was later, after the funeral and all, that I realized how hard their job must be. Not a job I could do. It obviously takes a special gift. I'll stick to my ghost-whispering gift; thank you very much. "Do you happen to know anything about the chaplain?" I ask.

"Whaddya mean?"

"I don't know exactly, like who were his friends? Did he have any enemies?"

"Enemies?" he laughs. "Everybody loved that guy."

"That's what I was afraid of," I sigh. When he looks at me strangely, I explain. "I'm just trying to figure out why someone would kill him."

"Ohh, gotcha. Sorry, I don't know of anyone."

"No problem. Thanks anyway," I tell him.

"Wait a minute!" he shouts after we start to walk away. "I can't believe I didn't think of dis before." He pauses like he's waiting to see what I do next.

"Go on!" I urge him.

"There was an orderly who worked here. Uhh, George, somethin' or other. The chaplain caught him stealing drugs and turned him in. Guy got fired on dah spot. Created dis huge scene. And get dis. The orderly screamed how he would kill him; den punched him right in dah kisser!"

"He punched the chaplain?" I gasp.

"Wait, *who* punched the chaplain?" Juliet asks.

Why do I always forget she can't hear the ghosts? "Some orderly got caught stealing drugs, threatened to kill the chaplain, then punched him."

"Right in dah kisser!" the ghost exclaims, punching the air.

"Right in dah kisser!" I repeat, swinging my own fist through the air.

Juliet steps back. "Whoa, there slugger."

"Sorry," I apologize. "Got caught up in the moment."

"Where do we find this orderly?" Juliet asks.

"I dunno." The ghost shrugs. "I just know it was the most excitement we seen here in a long time!"

"Do you know who could tell us where we might find him?" I ask.

He points to a girl behind the desk. "I think he and Tina were sweet on each other for a while. Ask her."

"We will. Thanks for your help," I tell him excitedly.

"Anytime, girls, anytime!" He waves as I bolt for the receptionist's desk.

"C'mon!" I signal a thoroughly confused Juliet to follow.

"Hi, excuse me, Tina?"

"Yes, how can I help you?"

"Could you tell me where to find George, the orderly you used to date?"

Her face clouds over. "Why do you want to know?" she asks warily.

"I'm a private investigator, and I'd like to talk to him."

She sighs. "Last I heard, he was bussing tables at Village Inn. But I don't know if he's still there. He probably got fired again. But if you see him, you didn't get any of that from me, okay?"

"Are you afraid of him?" I ask.

"Nah, not really, anyway." She shakes her head. "I just don't want to get caught up in a mess again. When he punched the chaplain, I almost got fired too. Especially when they realized he was stealing drugs. Do you know how many times I got called into HR on account of that loser? They even brought the cops in! I want nothing to do with him ever again. Actually, I wouldn't be surprised if he was dead."

"Overdose?" I ask.

"Overdose. Angry drug dealer. Who knows?"

"Do you think George could have killed the chaplain? You know, made good on his promise?"

"When George was high, he was capable of just about anything. You better watch your back if you confront him. When he's using, he has a nasty temper."

"Do you think we should tell Sheriff Mack about this?" Juliet asks. "What if this guy really is as dangerous as she says?"

She's probably right. I suppose we should fill in the sheriff, but how long will it take for the department to get around to interrogating the guy? I need this thing solved now.

"Let's pay this George a visit. If it looks dangerous, we'll leave immediately. I promise. Besides, can't you use witchcraft or something to save us?"

Juliet rolls her eyes. "There are a few things I can do if it becomes necessary. But it isn't foolproof."

"I'm sure we'll be fine. If we learn something important, then we'll go straight to Sheriff Mack."

"Okayyy," Juliet drawls. "I'm holding you to that."

Juliet is from East Texas, *right across the street from Louisiana*, she tells me. Her southern accent is slight, but it gets more pronounced when she's upset or angry.

Right now, I can tell she doesn't believe my offer to go to Sheriff Mack. That's okay. I'm serious—kind of.

12

"We forgot to ask them the most important question," I tell Juliet as we stare at the Village Inn sign.

"What's that?"

"How will we know which one is George?"

"Huh. Good point. I'm sure they can point us to him."

The parking lot is crowded for the day after Christmas. "This must be the town hot spot," I muse.

"Everybody working off their Christmas hangovers," Juliet offers. "Oh, you know what I want?"

"What?" I ask, confused. I hope she remembers we're here to confront a killer, not eat breakfast. Which may not be the best idea, now that I've had time to think about it. But there's strength in numbers, so if he gets violent, that could be our backup.

"Welcome to Village Inn! How many?" the chipper hostess asks. She obviously didn't overindulge on peppermint martinis last night.

"Two!" Juliet responds cheerfully.

"What are you doing?" I hiss in her ear. "We aren't here to eat."

"Don't you think it will be less suspicious if we're paying customers?" she hisses back defiantly.

"I suppose." I pause to consider her argument. Nope. Not buying it. "Hey, wait a minute, you just want breakfast!"

"But I'm hungry!"

"You own a bakery!" I remind her.

"We're closed today!"

"Fine. We'll eat breakfast *and* confront a killer."

The hostess regards us with a mixture of confusion and concern. No doubt we look like loons whisper-arguing about breakfast and killers. I give in and hold up two fingers.

"Great! This way, please."

My eyes dart to and fro as she escorts us to a table. A tall, skinny busboy passes by while I contort myself to look at his nametag. Sam. Dangit. Sam gives me a weird look.

If he thinks I'm off because of that, wouldn't he be surprised to know that there's a ghost sitting with a large, noisy family across the restaurant waving at me? I give him a simple head bob. I don't want the family to worry about the stranger in a crowded room waving at them.

"What'll it be, dears?" a pleasantly plump waitress with a silver bun on top of her head asks the moment we sit down. They're fast! No wonder this place is crowded.

"I'll have the steak and eggs, please," Juliet speaks up right away.

"Whoa. Eat much?" I ask before realizing how weird that might sound.

"Mind your own business much?" she retorts.

"Sorry!" I raise my hands in surrender. "I just meant that's a hearty breakfast for a small lady."

"Ha! Small. Tell my thighs that!" Juliet always fusses about her waistline. I think she's just right. Not too big. Not too small. Just right. Like Goldilocks porridge. Although I don't think she'd appreciate *that* comparison. She owns a bakery, after all. Who wants to see a skinny baker?

"And for you, miss?" the waitress sighs impatiently.

"Oops, sorry about that," I tell her, scanning the menu. "How about Huevos Rancheros?"

"Good choice," Juliet remarks.

"Coffee?' the waitress asks.

"Yes, please!" we tell her enthusiastically.

"I'll be right back with a fresh pot."

As soon as she leaves, Juliet leans forward. "See any George's yet?"

I shake my head. "We don't even know if he's working today."

"Or if he still works here," she reminds me.

Our heads snap to the side when a large young man bursts noisily from the kitchen door, clutching a large, empty dish bucket.

"Oh dear, why do I think that's him?" Juliet gulps.

"Because he's big enough to strangle someone?" I point out.

"Excuse me," Juliet queries when the waitress returns with our coffee.

"Is that George?" she asks, pointing to the young man clearing a table.

"You wanna talk to him?"

"If it's not too much trouble." I smile up at her.

"Hey George!" she shouts as several diners and George turn to stare. "These ladies want to talk to you!"

George lumbers in our direction. Er, we didn't really mean it like this, but okay.

"Hi," he says.

"Uh, hi," I start. What next? You'd think I'd learn to plan these things out beforehand, wouldn't you? It's just that I get so excited I run off half-cocked, as my dad liked to say, then I don't know where to go.

"Could we ask you some questions about Chaplain Palmer?"

"If you have the time!" Juliet adds.

At this, his face grows somber. He slumps down in the seat next to me. Ha! Caught him. Easy peasy lemon squeezy. He's prepared to give up already.

"I can't believe he's gone," he sighs, tears forming in his eyes.

Juliet and I look at each other. That's not what I expected.

"You seem sad," Juliet says gently.

"Of course, I'm sad," he sighs again, borrowing a napkin from one of the place settings. When he blows his nose loudly, I'm glad it isn't my napkin.

"We were told he got you fired, so you punched him."

"He did," he exclaims. "And I did!"

"So now you're sad that he died? I'm confused," Juliet says. "Or is it that you feel guilty?" Wow. Straight to the point, girl. Good for you.

"What? Guilty? No! He saved my life!" he exclaims.

"Come again?" Now *I'm* confused.

"Getting busted by the chaplain is the best thing that ever happened to me!" he exclaims.

Juliet's mouth forms an o.

"He saved my life that day. Well, after I punched him anyway. He showed up at my place later, said he forgave me, and that I could go to rehab or jail. It was my choice. I realized that if a guy I just assaulted could care that much, then maybe I should too." He digs around in his front pocket. "Check it out! I got my 90-day sober chip on Christmas Eve! Kind of appropriate, don't you think?"

"That's great! Congratulations!" I tell him, trying to keep the disappointment from my voice. Don't get me wrong; I'm genuinely happy for the guy. I get it. Conquering your demons. Starting over. I *so* get it. But he was my only suspect. Unless I count Gabriel, but I'm not ready to count him yet. Now we're back to square one.

"Breakfast is served, gals!" the waitress announces when she arrives with our food.

"I better get back to work!" George says, jumping up from his chair. "You guys have a good day!"

"One more thing!" I tell him before he leaves. "I have to ask; where were you around 11 PM last night?"

"I was at a meeting, of course! I can have my sponsor give you a call if you want. I mean, you're with the police, right? I kind of figured you'd come by here."

Juliet smiles and says, "Mmm."

So, we didn't really lie to the guy, did we? "I feel bad for being momentarily disappointed that he doesn't hate the chaplain like I thought he would," I admit to Juliet.

"You were hoping we could solve this quickly. Believe me, so was I."

"Hey, one more thing." George hurries back to our table. "I probably shouldn't be repeating this, but I want you to catch whoever did this."

We lean forward in anticipation.

"I overheard some guys talking at a meeting recently. You know, AA," he explains when we look lost. "It turns out the reason the chaplain knew exactly what I needed, was that he too, was an addict. A gambler, from what these guys were saying."

"You think the chaplain was gambling?" I interrupt.

"Nah, from what I understand, he's been sober a long time. But," he holds his finger in the air, "his old bookie never got over the chaplain going on the straight and narrow. He's come back to town recently and was harassing him. These guys said Chaplain Palmer planned to take it to the sheriff once the holidays were over."

"It sounds like this could be worth pursuing. Where do I find this guy?" I ask George.

13

—— ◆ ——

On our way back to Wendy's bookstore, I notice I missed a call from Professor Jonas Lawson, a geology professor at Colorado Mountain College. I initially called him when the peridot disappeared last summer, even though I'm not exactly sure how he can help me. But he specializes in gems found in the Colorado mountains, so I didn't think it would hurt to ask about the peridot's background.

Only he was out of the country when I called, so I left a message and I have to admit I kind of forgot about him until just now. I'm glad he's back, though. After I drop Juliet off at the bookstore, I head to CMC.

"Hi Professor, I'm Holly Daniel."

"Holly, yes, so good to meet you. You're here about the stolen peridot?" I was hoping he'd look like Indiana Jones because how fun would that be? But if I'm being honest, he looks more like Professor Jennings from Animal House. Minus the pot smell.

"Yes, the mayor hired me to find it."

"I can't say I'm surprised it was stolen. They left it just sitting on that pedestal, with visitors coming and going, all day, every day. What does shock me is that it's taken this long."

"You don't believe that witchcraft protected it?"

He snorts. "I am a scientist. I believe in science. I think that the town's founder saved a woman from the railroad tracks, so she gave him a large peridot to thank him. I think *she* believed she could guard it with a spell, but I *know* there's no scientific basis to this. Meanwhile, a bunch of gullible folks have believed this story for over 100 years, leaving the stone untouched. Finally, last summer, somebody who can actually think for themselves, stole it."

"You almost sound like you're a fan," I point out.

"No, not at all. He *or* she stole something that didn't belong to them. I don't support that at all. I'm merely saying I appreciate someone who doesn't believe in fairy tales."

"What about all the bad things that have happened in Glenwood since the stone was stolen?" I ask.

"Don't tell me *you* believe the stone has magical powers?"

"My personal beliefs aren't important here," I say as gently as I can. "I'm the investigator, after all. I'm just curious about your theories."

"Fair enough," he responds thoughtfully. "There's no rule that says bad or good luck, so to speak, has to occur in even doses. If the town experienced what appeared to be a run of good fortune, I suspect we'd barely notice. But now that the town has undergone several *un*fortunate events, everyone is desperate for answers. A stolen gem believed to somehow protect the town is an easy answer. It may be human nature to crave these things, but it's not scientific."

"Have you heard anything in your professional circles about it?"

"There's been some discussion and even some rumors. It's famous, after all. Do you think a geologist stole it?"

"At this point, I'm willing to investigate any avenue. It's like it just disappeared without a trace. Even Ronald Thurman, the retired jewel thief, has heard nothing from the usual suspects," I explain.

"None of my colleagues have admitted to stealing it, if that's what you're wondering."

"Bummer. That would make my day a lot easier," I laugh.

"Do you have a lot of cases you're investigating right now?"

"With the chaplain's murder last night, I've taken on that as well. At least unofficially," I lament.

"Someone was murdered? Here?" he exclaims in shock.

"Yes, I'm surprised you haven't heard about it; it's all over the news."

"I just got back, and I'm still pretty jet lagged, so I've paid little attention to the news," he says.

"They found Chaplain Palmer's body behind the Red Castle Hotel last night. He was strangled." At this point, I don't think I need to tell him *who* found him. I'd prefer to keep that under wraps as much as possible. Too many people will want to remind me this is my second body, and I haven't even lived here for a year.

"Hmm. The name doesn't ring a bell," he admits.

"He was the chaplain at the nursing home and the hospital."

"Ah, got it. I've never visited either of those places. Do they have any suspects yet?"

"It's all over the news, so I might as well tell you. Their main suspect is the manager at the Red Castle Hotel."

"They've arrested someone already?"

"No, they haven't arrested him, but he's their primary target, from what I understand."

"Huh. Can't say I know him either. I'm sorry; I wish I could be more helpful to you. With both your cases."

"Before I go, could you give me a little background on the peridot gem?" I ask.

"What I know to be true, or what people believe about them?"

"Both."

"It might surprise you to learn that these days, most of the peridot comes from Arizona on the San Carlos Apache Indian Reservation. But the first recorded mining was in 300 B.C. in Egypt. While many believe Cleopatra was famous for emeralds, they were more likely peridot."

"When I saw the Precious Peridot in the museum, it surprised me how beautiful it was," I tell him.

"I've seen it too. It's breathtaking. What I wouldn't have done to hold it before it was stolen," he says wistfully.

"Is it just our Precious Peridot that people think has special powers, or do they think all of them have mystical qualities?" I ask.

"Oh, my dear, since the beginning of civilization, people have convinced themselves that all peridot have special qualities other than physical beauty. Ancient civilizations believed it could help with creativity and awareness. Still others insisted it could ward off nightmares."

"But as you've assured me, you don't believe that," I remind him.

"That a gem could offer magical properties to protect an entire town and quell nightmares? Correct. I don't believe that. But that doesn't make it any less valuable. Not to me, anyway. In fact, when you find it, I'd be ever so grateful for the chance to hold it. If that's possible. It would be the opportunity of a lifetime for this geologist."

I shrug. "It's not up to me, but I'll certainly ask the mayor about it."

"Perhaps once you locate the gem, the mayor will be so happy she'll grant you a special favor," he responds hopefully.

"I appreciate your confidence," I tell him. "As thanks, I will tell the mayor I have a special request."

"Splendid!" he cries.

—◆—

14

I glare daggers at Billy "The Bulldozer" Bishop across the bar while drying a snifter glass so hard a nearby ghost asks me if I'm trying to break it on purpose. When George told me the bookie's name who was threatening the chaplain, I didn't need to ask where to find him.

Unfortunately, he often meets his so-called customers in the hotel bar, along with what I and many others suspect are mobsters. He and Gabriel butt heads regularly. Gabriel doesn't want him meeting people here, knowing they're conducting illegal business. Billy the Bulldozer insists that he's a legitimate businessman meeting with investors.

Of course, he's legit. Don't all businessmen earn a nickname based on how they dispose of their enemy's bodies? Mr. Sinclair, the previous manager, didn't like it either, but he was too afraid of Billy to do anything about it. Gabriel insists they don't scare him.

I worry he may be messing with the wrong people. I don't like having them in my bar either, but I don't want to be on their hit list. What if Billy made good on his threats to kill Chaplain Palmer?

I think that's a better possibility than *Gabriel* killing him. Although Gabriel promised me a few weeks ago that he'd get rid of Billy and his henchmen once and for all. Now I kind of wonder about that.

Look at him over there, I mutter under my breath. Yucking it up with his mobster friends, talking and laughing so loudly that some customers throw salty looks his way. He makes money off people's misery yet acts like he hasn't a care in the world.

That's it! I think angrily when he smacks a passing waitress on her backside. I slam the glass on the counter, along with my dish towel next to it, and march toward their table. I'm tired of their antics. I'm confronting them right now. If Gabriel isn't afraid of them, neither am I.

15

— · —

I get halfway there when someone grabs me from behind, pulling me back toward the bar. "What the..." I sputter. It's Sheriff Mack. Why must he appear at the most inopportune times? "Let me go!" I insist.

"I know what you're planning, and I won't let you," he whispers in my ear.

"Oh, and what's that?" I respond angrily.

"You've had enough of them," he nods his head toward the mobsters who seem oblivious to our argument, "so you decided to do something about it. On top of that, you think he could be the chaplain's murderer."

I sputter some more because I can't think of a good argument to refute his accusation.

"That's what I thought," he continues. "Is there somewhere we can talk?" he asks, nodding his head again toward the mobsters.

"Will the kitchen do?"

"That's fine."

When the sheriff and I enter the kitchen, Jerry squints at us and tsks like he can't believe we're interrupting his work again.

"Sorry, Jerry." I shrug.

"Holly, you can't mess with those guys." Sheriff Mack waggles his finger in my face.

"I'm not messing with them. It's just that I heard Billy threatened the chaplain for convincing too many people to stop gambling. If you ask me, that makes him a suspect."

"I don't care what it makes him. If you think you know so much, do you know his nickname?"

"It's Bulldozer."

"That's right--"

"Before you ask," I interrupt, holding my hand up, "I also know how he got the nickname."

"Yet you think it's perfectly acceptable to stomp up to him to tell him off?"

"There's other people in the bar. It's not like he could do anything to me without a dozen witnesses filming the entire thing on their phones."

"It's not what he'd do to you in the middle of the bar that I'm worried about. It's what he'd do when you're driving home late at night where there are no witnesses that worries me."

Gulp. He's got me there.

"I know you're eager to clear your *friend's* name--"

"He's my *boss*." I interrupt again.

"Whatever. I know you're eager to clear *his* name, but you must be careful here."

"I know, I know. Let the professionals handle it." I mock.

"That's exactly it. How about this? I actually need your help this time."

"Really? Or are you just trying to distract me?"

"I really think you can be helpful," he says.

"Okay, shoot."

"I need you to ask your ghost friends to keep an eye on Billy for me. Notice I didn't say *you*. I mean it. It must be your other-worldly friends that do this. I don't want you anywhere near Billy, got it? Because the ghosts have helped us in the past, I thought they might be willing to do it again?"

"I can ask. Anything specific in mind?"

"Ask them to watch him and listen in on his conversations. I want to know if he mentions the chaplain. Or even if he admits to something illegal."

"You want them to report back to me if he admits to *any* crime, killing the chaplain or otherwise?"

"Precisely. I know your friend, I mean, your boss has been itching to get rid of them. I wouldn't mind seeing them disappear myself. Although preferably to jail. We know they're mobsters; we know they're into gambling and theft, plus murder, of course, but we haven't been able to pin anything on them. If your ghosts could lurk about sight unseen, one of those clowns might say something in front of them that would provide us with leads."

I nod vigorously. "That's actually an excellent idea, Sheriff!"

"You seem surprised," he says with a smirk.

I shrug. "I'm just so used to you lecturing me. It's unusual for you to ask for my help."

"Perhaps you should stop doing things that require lectures."

"I don't see that happening," I tell him.

He starts to say something further but thinks better of it. I'm sure he's tired of arguing with me. "I'll go out the back door. I don't want Billy to see us together again and get suspicious. If you need anything, you call me. And stay away from Billy!"

"Will do!" I salute him while he shakes his head at my antics and slips out the back door.

It wasn't necessary, anyway. When I return to the bar, Billy and his ilk are gone. Most of the patrons have cleared out for the night as well. I post the sign on the counter that says we'll return first thing tomorrow morning, should anyone need a Bloody Mary. I carefully fold my apron and place it on a shelf, preparing to leave.

When I notice the light is on in Gabriel's office, I remember that I still haven't discussed the chaplain's murder with him. *It's now or never*, I tell myself as I square my shoulders, marching into his office. "Hey Gabriel, how's it going?"

"Well, let's see, I'm the primary suspect in a good man's murder, I was hit in the head with a brick, and the Sheriff's Department is watching my every move. Other than that, it's going great. How about you?"

"I still haven't found the Precious Peridot, and now I'm investigating Chaplain Palmer's murder."

"Let me guess. You want to know where I was when the chaplain was murdered?"

I grimace. "Is it that obvious?"

"It's what everyone is asking." He shrugs.

An uncomfortable silence settles over us. "So, where were you?" I press.

He looks confused. "I was at the party. You saw me. I asked you about your Christmas, and we had a drink," he reminds me.

When he says this, I feel uneasy. A sensation I try desperately to ignore. I'm probably just paranoid, but what if he did that on purpose? Was he trying to give himself a very public alibi? I recall how everyone was staring at us.

"Well, yes," I admit. "But that was before the chaplain was killed, right?" I can't believe I'm actually arguing with my boss about an alibi for a murder. "I have to point out that many other people saw you walk back through the ballroom *after* you talked to me. You were disheveled and sporting a scratch on your face that wasn't there before."

I point to my cheek. "It's still scratched. You also appeared to come from the employee entrance, where they found the chaplain. You have to know how suspicious that looks."

Gabriel stares at me unblinkingly. The clock on the wall ticks loudly. Counting down the seconds, or has it been minutes? This is the first time I've noticed that clock. Now it mocks me. Ticking down the moments before my boss fires me for being so disrespectful.

When he finally breaks the silence, it's so sudden it startles me. "I'm also the new guy in town, and if the rumors are true, I'm a freak of nature, so how could I not be guilty, right?"

"That's not what I meant at all," I protest.

"It's what everyone is saying."

"I know," I murmur.

I don't quite know what to say to him. That overall, my experience in this town has been fabulous? Sure, there were the hiccups with the stolen tiara, then Mr. Beasley's murder, but it's not like those were my fault. "I don't know you that well, but you certainly don't *seem* like a murderer," I tell him.

"Gee, thanks."

Darn, that didn't sound like I wanted it to. I'll start over. "I seriously doubt that you killed Chaplain Palmer."

He crooks an eyebrow. This still isn't going as I hoped. "Part of the reason I decided to investigate Chaplain Palmer's murder was that I think some people in this town are judging you unfairly. I know personally what that's like. I don't think you killed the chaplain, or anybody else for that matter."

"If you must know, I was in the storage building behind the hotel looking for a ladder." He points to the ceiling. "The fluorescent light bulb was flickering all day and driving me crazy. The janitorial staff had the day off for Christmas, but I figured I could replace it myself. I just needed a ladder. When I got to the storage building, I fumbled for the light switch, tripped, fell against some shelving, and banged myself up. It's embarrassing, really. I hurried through the ballroom, hoping no one would notice and ask me what happened."

It certainly sounds reasonable, but why don't I believe him?

16

Wendy, Juliet, and I file somberly into the nursing home for the memorial service for Chaplain Palmer the following morning. It's a bitter cold morning with gray skies and spitting snow. Appropriate funeral weather.

I've been to my share of funerals but never for a murder victim. There's an especially dark aura surrounding the building right now. It's a nursing home, so there's also a lot of ghosts lurking about. And even they seem melancholy right now.

The crowd is too big to fit into the tiny chapel, so they moved the service to the cafeteria. The staff pushed the round dining tables against the wall and into corners while the plastic chairs, all a charming shade of harvest gold, sit in neat rows. Flowers from well-wishers line the walls. The smell of that many flowers packed into one room is sickeningly sweet. The whole thing is especially depressing.

I barely remember Ben's funeral. The Honor Guard was there, of course, to present me with a flag. The three-volley salute had everyone around me jumping in their seats. I barely noticed it. There were so many of Ben's battle buddies in attendance it was almost overwhelming. Yet I was grateful for their company.

George is sitting alone across the room. When he waves to us, we wave back. I haven't entirely written him off as a suspect. I make a mental note to follow up on his alibi. Sheriff Mack once told me that he always attends the funeral because the killer often shows up as well.

I didn't believe him at first, but he claims that sometimes they're worried they may have left something behind and are about to be caught. Still others regret what they did and attend the funeral out of guilt. If that's the case, maybe I'll get lucky, and we'll catch the killer today.

The pastor from a local church is conducting the service. It's a traditional service with prayers and some hymns. At the end, he invites anyone who would like to share a memory to approach the lectern.

Numerous people tell stories about how the chaplain changed their lives. Many comment on how he was there for them in their greatest time of need. More than one former gambler tells the story of how the chaplain saved their families and their lives by convincing them to get help for their addiction. Everyone loved this guy. George nods enthusiastically for all of them.

When it appears the sharing is complete, the pastor asks one last time if there's anyone else who wants to share. If not, there's a luncheon reception in the rec room.

Thank goodness. I'm getting hungry and could really go for a sandwich. This was a nice way to honor the chaplain. While there were plenty of tears there was a lot of laughter and smiles as well.

But just when we think we're all ready to head to the reception, a man stumbles to the front. Murmurs ripple through the crowd. The guy is obviously drunk.

"This should be good," Wendy whispers.

The man clutches the lectern attempting to steady himself.

"I killed the chaplain!" he proclaims.

17

—·—

"What?" Wendy shouts in disbelief.

Juliet and I stare at her. I can't believe she just shouted that. Although I almost did the same. Who is this guy? Is he serious? I don't recognize him. Where did he come from?

Chatter spreads through the crowd as everyone talks at once. The pastor is exceptionally uncomfortable. I bet this is a first for him!

Sheriff Mack appears concerned, but I notice he's not getting up to arrest the guy.

"Just kidding!" he laughs. "I meant I *wanted* to kill him." He then clutches the sides of the podium, leaning forward to stare at the crowd. "I bet you're all wondering why I wanted to kill him, aren't you?"

Most of us stare back in shock. A few people nod, though, as if he were asking a serious question.

Everyone's head swivels when a young woman from the back of the room, wearing a stylish black dress, marches to the front. Her high heels clack loudly on the tile floor.

"Ethan!" she scolds. "Stop this nonsense right now! Our mother would be ashamed of you." As soon as she reaches him, she grabs his arm to pull him away, but he jerks it back.

"No, Sylvia! These people need to know. Your beloved Chaplain Palmer," he angrily jabs his finger at the crowd, "talked my mother into giving all her money to him. That was my money!" he shouts.

Lunch is forgotten while we watch the drama playing out in front of us. The two siblings continue to argue, while no one seems to know what to do. Should we leave and let them argue in private? Should we try to break up the argument? It's clear that some people want to stay and watch the fight.

The pastor finally approaches them for a quiet conversation. Then he signals to an usher from the mortuary who hurries forward to escort Ethan and Sylvia to the chairs against the wall. Sylvia insists her brother sit down while a nurse hands him a bottle of water.

Well, that was unexpected. How often does a suspect just land in my lap like that? He may be drunk, but he obviously has it in for the chaplain. And money can be a powerful motivation for murder. I need to find out who he is and interrogate him. Once he sobers up, that is.

The ushers from the mortuary urge the rest of us to head to the rec room for lunch, but no one wants to leave. We can't seem to take our eyes off the pair of siblings who are still arguing. At least they've toned it down to more of a dull roar now.

We're all waiting for Ethan to say more. Did the beloved chaplain really steal his mother's money? Did he use undue influence on her? If so, are the others? There would have to be, right? The suspects could be endless.

I also want to know where he was when the chaplain was killed. I don't recall seeing him at the Christmas party, but there were so many people there I can't recall everyone who attended.

Eventually, the crowd files out of the cafeteria and into the rec room for cold-cut sandwiches, potato salad, and baked beans. The nursing home staff said it was the chaplain's favorite lunch. For dessert, we had devil's food cupcakes with cream cheese frosting.

After lunch, a man who works at the train station, and whose name always escapes me, corners me to tell me all about how much he misses fishing in the winter.

He explains in great detail the intricacies of how to catch rainbow trout in the Colorado River. I'm sure if I were interested in fishing, this story would be fascinating, but all I can think about at this point is how to escape.

As I scan the room for a reason to excuse myself, I notice an elderly woman in the corner staring at me. She's wearing a long floral print dress; her silver hair is tied back in a ponytail. She's also wearing a paper wrist tag, so I assume she's a nursing home resident. But why is she staring at me?

I'm so tired of pretending to care what Boring Fish Guy says I think if I just walked away, he wouldn't even notice. He'd just keep droning on. What I really need to do is get out of here so I can check into this Ethan character.

I turn in a circle, desperately searching for Wendy and Juliet to see if they're ready to leave. When I turn back around, the fisherman is still talking, and the elderly woman is gone.

"Psst!" a woman whispers from behind me.

I spin back around. It's her!

"Me?"

"Yes, you!"

"How many are there?" she asks.

"Excuse me?"

"I know you can see them. This place must be chock full of em'. Am I right?" she exclaims.

I consider playing dumb, but I don't want to be inconsiderate. She must be a witch or some other type of paranormal being. The first time I met Wendy, she could tell immediately that I was a spirit communicator.

I nod. "Yes, there are quite a few spirits here."

"Have you seen my son?" she asks.

How sad. Her son must have passed. Although I doubt it was in this building.

"What is your son's name?" I ask gently. Anything to get away from the fisherman.

"His name is Herbert." She pauses, looking lost. "Wait, my nephew's name is Herbert too."

"I'm so sorry. Was it your son that passed? Or your nephew?" This is a confusing conversation.

"No, not passed. Have you seen him?"

"I don't understand." Oh, dear. This is going nowhere fast, and I don't know what to do.

"I asked if you've seen my son!" she shouts, growing more agitated by the moment. I scan the room, hoping for assistance. I don't know what to do.

"Mildred, let's get you back to your room," a nurse says, rushing over to us. "She's a resident of our Alzheimer's wing. She's not supposed to be out here."

"Oh, that's too bad. She keeps asking about her son. Did he pass?"

Now the nurse is confused. "She never had a son."

"Huh, okay."

"I'm sorry, but I need to get her back to her room immediately, before she gets any worse."

"Yes, of course."

"Wait!" Mildred shouts, struggling to get away from the nurse. "I have something special for you!" She holds out her fist as if she has something in it when there clearly wasn't just a few moments ago.

I look at the nurse for direction.

"It's this thing she does." She shakes her head. "Just hold out your hand."

I do as I'm told while Mildred pretends to place something in my hand.

"Rats!" she says when she sees my empty hand. "I just had it."

"Mildred, sweetie, we need to go back now."

"Fine," Mildred mutters. "I want my lunch!"

"You already had lunch," the nurse reassures her.

"So, when's dinner?"

I watch them walk away while Mildred continues to question the nurse about her meal schedule. I can't imagine what that would be like. That poor woman.

"Hey, you, are you ready to go?" Wendy asks, suddenly appearing at my side.

"Yes! I am so ready to go!" I tell her.

"Who was that?" Juliet nods toward Mildred and the nurse.

"Mildred." I shrug. "She must be a witch because she knew I could see dead people. She even asked about her son."

"That's awful. She must have thought you could see her son's spirit," Wendy says.

"I guess." I shrug. "But my next task is to find that guy who said he killed the chaplain."

"You don't think he really killed him, do you?" Wendy asks. "He certainly wouldn't announce it to a room full of people, after all."

"I don't know, but I intend to find out."

18

"That's so shiny; I bet if I weren't transparent, I could see myself in it!" Fiona exclaims while watching me polish the bar top. I love how elegant this place is. The bar itself is a chocolatey brown color with dark brown streaks marbled throughout. They tell me it's walnut.

A red brick archway leads from the lobby into the bar with a sparkling chandelier lighting the way. The carpet is so thick I swear someday I'm going to go barefoot just so I can squish my toes in it.

Fiona hovers over the top of the bar anyway, just to double-check. "Nope. Still can't see myself. So, what did you want to talk to me about?"

I put my finger over my lips while motioning to a group of people across the room. I don't want to risk anyone overhearing me asking Fiona to spy on the mafia. When the group leaves a few minutes later, I motion to her to come back. "I need a favor," I tell her.

"Oh, goody!" she cries, waving around her luminescent arms.

Fiona was one of the first ghosts I met when I started working in the hotel. I still feel bad about the way I treated her. She was so eager to have a live person to talk to. But I was too busy pursuing my own agenda that I blew her off. To my detriment. I'll never do that again! "This request actually came from Sheriff Mack," I explain.

"Yippie! He's quite attractive, don't you think?"

Oh, brother. She sounds like Clara. Sometimes I wonder if I should tell the sheriff about his spirit fan club. Let him know he has a way with the ghost gals. Nah. I fear it would just make him more obnoxious than ever. Though I suspect if these ladies had to work with him the same way I do, they wouldn't be so keen on him.

"Yeah, he's super handsome, whatever, here's what I need you to do." Fiona hovers close. "You know Billy Bishop I assume?"

"You mean the mobster?" she asks, scrunching her face with disgust.

"That's the one."

"He's a very bad man. I hope you aren't messing with him. He's dangerous."

"I know that. That's why I need your help. Have you ever heard him admit to a crime?"

She shakes her head vigorously. "I try my best to stay away from them. I hate that they come in here."

"So do I. And so does Gabriel."

"Mmm, he's another handsome one." She nods appreciatively.

What is it with these ghosts? "Remind me not to introduce him to Clara, then."

"Huh?"

"Nothing. Anyway, as I was saying, you're not the only one who wants to get rid of them. Sheriff Mack has a special request. He'd like you and the other ghosts to listen in on their conversations."

"We can do that!" she exclaims. "Is there anything in particular you want us to listen for?"

"I think they're suspects in the chaplain's murder."

"Really? The sheriff thinks it's Gabriel. I still say he's too handsome to kill anyone," she purrs, batting her eyelashes while clutching her hands to her heart.

"You weren't murdered by a serial killer by any chance, were you?"

"Huh? No. I got drunk at a holiday party, passed out in the courtyard fountain, and drowned."

"What? That's awful! Why didn't you tell me that before?"

"You never asked." She shrugs.

Now I feel bad again. I really need to have longer conversations with those in the spirit world. They probably have some fascinating stories, but I usually think I'm too busy. But I'm a bartender, for pete's sake. And a private investigator. I'm supposed to listen to people. Living or otherwise.

"I'll tell the others right now!" she says, preparing to zoom away.

"Oh, wait! One more thing!" I shout as she pauses. "Is there a ghost here by the name of Herbert, by any chance?"

She shakes her head. "Not that I know of. Why do you ask?"

"No big deal. Just wondering."

"Oh, okay, well, I'll go tell the others."

"Thanks!"

Then, as if we summoned the devil himself, Billy and several of his minions stroll into the bar wearing *cat ate the canary* expressions. Knowing them, they probably did.

I almost send a waitress over to their table when I think better of it. I'll handle them myself. If someone dares to smack me on the backside, I'll bean him over the head with a serving tray. Mobsters or not, they don't get to treat people like that.

"Hey, good lookin'!" a chubby mobster with glasses and a toupee says.

"What can I get you, gentlemen, this evening?" I ask, nearly gagging at the word, gentlemen.

"Are your eyes really that color or are those contacts?" a stocky mobster with a shaved head asks.

"They're really that color," I sigh.

"I'll have an extra dry martini with two olives," the third mobster tells me.

"Great." I scribble that down. "And for the rest of you?"

I catch chubby reaching for me out of the corner of my eye. Quick as a wink, I smack his hand with my serving tray. "Please keep your hands to yourself," I growl.

"Ohhh, she got you good!" Bald guy shrieks with laughter while the others laugh with him.

My heart rate spikes when chubby jumps out of his seat, putting his face inches from mine.

"No one disrespects Joey!" he shouts.

"Do you always refer to yourself in the third person?" I bite back while the others continue to howl with laughter. Oh boy, now I've really done it. I'm about two seconds from kneeing this guy in the family jewels and running when Billy slams his hand on the table, making us all jump.

"Enough!" he shouts. "Joey, sit down!" Joey immediately drops back into his chair. "Apologize to this young woman for treating her like a piece of meat."

"Sorry," Joey mumbles.

"I'm terribly sorry, miss. He was raised in a barn. Please forgive him."

I give Billy a curt nod. I'm not buying his polite act, either. But I don't need to push this further. Sheriff Mack would be furious if he saw what I just did. I couldn't help myself. These guys are scum.

"Remember, boys, we're here to celebrate tonight. Miss, your best champagne, please."

I don't ask what they're celebrating. I'm sure I don't want to know, anyway.

"Hey, do I still get my martini?" the third mobster asks.

"Yes, you can still have your martini," Billy grumbles.

"Good! I love them little olives," he exclaims.

Billy rolls his eyes. "Your best champagne and an extra dry martini for the doofus here."

"Coming right up," I tell them. I'm sure they all watch me as I walk away. I'm so tempted to flip them off, but for once, I heed the sheriff's previous warning and behave myself. I hope Fiona overhears them confessing to killing the chaplain, and they'll soon be in jail.

I wonder if they're celebrating the chaplain's demise, considering we just had the memorial service. Now I'm madder than ever. I'll tell Fiona to put a rush on their eavesdropping. The sooner they're gone, the better.

While I make the careful trek back to the mobster's table with their champagne and martini, a ghost named Toby rushes into the bar.

"Come quick! You won't believe what's happening out here!" he exclaims.

"What now?" I blurt out.

"Excuse me?" Billy says.

"Oh, nothing, sorry, I was just talking to myself." I quickly place the bucket of ice, bottle of champagne, four champagne coupes, and the martini in front of them. Normally I'd ask if the customer needs anything else, but where these guys are concerned, I don't care.

Besides, Toby looks like he's ready to wet his pants if I don't rush to see what he's bellowing about. If ghosts could wet their pants, that is. I chase after Toby into the hotel lobby, where I skid to a halt. Sheriff Mack is there, along with about a half dozen of his deputies.

"What's going on?" I exclaim. Is there a bomb threat? Or a fire? What could require this kind of police presence? Then I realize Sheriff Mack is handcuffing my boss.

"Gabriel Molina, you're under arrest for the murder of Christopher Palmer."

19

—— ● ——

This can't be happening. "Why are you arresting him?" I cry. "Do you have any evidence? Or are you just discriminating against him?"

Sheriff Mac shoots me the angriest look I've ever seen him give me. And that's saying something! "The department doesn't comment on ongoing investigations," he snarls.

"But I need to know!" I insist. Why won't anyone listen to me? They just keep pushing me aside. "Do you have any specific evidence?"

"Holly, I swear to you. I didn't kill the chaplain. You have to believe me," Gabriel begs. Fear consumes his face as the deputies lead him out the door to the waiting patrol car.

After I watch them drive away, I wander back into the bar area in a daze, racking my brain over how this could happen. What convinced the sheriff's department to arrest him now? What changed?

Billy and his pals look especially smug right now. I'm positive they had something to do with it. It's way too coincidental for them to be here at this exact time, bragging about how they're celebrating. They are overly boisterous tonight, and I've run out of patience with these clowns. I'm getting answers right now.

"Holly, wait!" Toby's form floats in front of me. Obviously, he can't block my path, but it's enough to distract me for a moment.

"Can't it wait? I have business to attend to," I snap at him.

"I have important news for you."

"Fine, lay it on me."

"I overheard the sheriff's deputies talking outside. The medical examiner found DNA evidence under the chaplain's fingernails."

"Let me guess, it belonged to Gabriel," I respond, sinking into the nearest chair, my knees suddenly weak from the shock.

Toby nods reluctantly. He doesn't want to believe this any more than I do. "The scratch," I murmur, pointing to my face as I flashback to Gabriel, telling me he fell against some shelving in the dark. I know I said I didn't believe him at the time, but that didn't mean I thought he was the killer. But if they have DNA evidence, how could he be anything other than the killer?

When I see a customer waiting patiently at the bar, I snap out of my daze and hurry over to serve her. I'm still on duty, after all.

"Dude, I'm really scared that I'll get in trouble with that sheriff guy if he finds out I lied about George not being here during the Christmas party."

I'm so shocked when I hear that, I drop the pitcher I'm washing. It shatters into about a million pieces. The two young men, whispering next to the bar, spin around to see what the commotion is. I know they work in the dining room, but I don't know their names.

"You, okay?" the tall one with tattoos asks.

"Yeah, yeah, I'm fine, just clumsy," I assure him. But I need to know more. "I'm really sorry to bother you guys, but could you get a broom from the storage closet? I don't want anyone to get hurt," I whine, hoping my helpless female act will do the trick. After all, it's worked in the past.

"Sure thing!" They jump up, fighting over who can get to the closet first.

When they return, I bat my eyes at them again. "Can you help me clean up too? Be careful! The glass is sharp!"

"Aww, we'll be fine," the one with big ears and a beard insists.

"Did you say you lied to the sheriff? I promise I won't tell." I ask, my eyes round with what I hope looks like wonder and awe. "I'd be afraid to lie to him. He's scary, don't you think?"

"He's not that big of a deal," Big Ears says, puffing out his chest.

"Okay, now I have to know." I playfully swat at Tall Guy with the dish towel. "What did you say to the sheriff? I promise I won't tell."

"Welll..." Big Ears responds while they look at each other nervously.

"C'mon, it will be our secret. I like secrets." Barf. I'm making myself nauseous.

"Fine. You have to swear you won't tell," Tall Guy insists.

"I promise!" I cross my heart to show them how serious I am. That's still a thing, right?

"The sheriff interrogated our friend George after they found the chaplain. Did you know he assaulted him once and even threatened to kill him?"

"No way!" I exclaim.

"Way, dude," Big Ears says earnestly. "When the sheriff asked George if he was at the Christmas party, he lied and said he wasn't."

It takes every single little bit of willpower I have not to shriek *what*? "Really?" I respond as calmly as I possibly can. "Why did he lie?"

"He had to. Otherwise, it might look like he killed the guy after they argued."

"They argued? Here? During the Christmas party?" I dig my fingernails into the palms of my hands so hard I'm sure they're bleeding. I have to keep calm. I'm so close to learning that George killed Chaplain Palmer, I can taste it.

"Yeah, man, right out back. It got ugly, too," Tall Guy says.

"What time did they argue?" I ask a little too eagerly.

"I'm not sure." He shrugs.

"It was pretty late, like 10 or 11, maybe?" Big Ears offers.

I knew it! I want to shout. That story about the chaplain saving him was malarkey. "You're sure he lied to the sheriff?"

"Uhhh, yeah. Why are you so interested in this all of a sudden?" Big Ears asks, his tone growing suspicious.

"Oh, I'm not. Not really. I was just curious, that's all. It gets pretty boring around here, you know. At least it's a little excitement, right?"

"Yeah, that it is." He nods appreciatively.

"You guys don't think George could have killed the chaplain, do you?"

"Nah!" Tall Guy says.

"I'm not so sure, bro; remember the time he completely trashed the pinball machine in that bar in Rifle because it ate his quarter? I thought those people were going to shoot us!"

"Oh! I forgot about that!" Big Ears recalls fondly. "That argument on Christmas looked pretty intense, didn't it?"

"It looked?" I ask.

"We couldn't hear them that well, but when George stomped off, he was furious."

So, George lied about his alibi. According to these guys, anyway; he also asked them to lie about a fight that must have happened right before the chaplain was killed. Or should I say right before *he* killed the chaplain?

"What did you guys do after you saw George leave?"

"Hey, you're not with the cops or anything, are you?" Tall Guy asks. Now they're both nervous.

"Me? Nah, I'm just a bartender."

"Okay, because if George knew we were blabbing to the cops, he'd be steamed."

"Your secret's safe with me, guys." At least until I get off work. *Hang on, boss; you may be out of jail sooner than you think.*

20

— • —

I sip my coffee, waiting for my bagel to toast while Clara reads the newspaper and Mystery perches on the windowsill, slowly swishing her fluffy tail.

"I can't believe they arrested your boss!" Clara exclaims, pointing to the picture in the newspaper. "He's certainly a handsome one, isn't he? Why didn't you tell me that before?"

What is it with these ghosts? "To be fair, he's been the primary suspect all along, so I guess it's not that surprising they arrested him," I point out.

"But you told me you thought he was innocent."

"I still mostly think that."

"Do you know why they finally arrested him? The paper didn't say."

"Toby, one of the ghosts at the hotel, told me he overheard a deputy saying they found Gabriel's DNA under the chaplain's fingernails."

"That's bad. Do you think that's how he got the scratch?" Clara asked.

"It makes more sense than him falling against a shelf in the dark."

"So now you think he killed the chaplain?" Mystery says.

"I don't know what to think at this point. But how do you argue with that kind of evidence?"

"He scratched Gabriel, but someone else strangled him?" Clara suggests.

"That seems far-fetched."

"Gabriel had an accomplice who strangled the chaplain?" Mystery adds.

"That still makes him guilty, though."

"Do you have any more leads? Have you talked to anyone else?" Clara asks.

"Remember George, the guy from the Village Inn?"

"The one the chaplain got fired?"

"Yes. His friends told me last night that he asked them to lie about where he was on Christmas night."

"Why would he do that?" Mystery asks.

"Because he was at the Christmas party and got into a heated argument with the chaplain, then stormed off."

Clara gasps. "You think he came back and strangled the chaplain?"

"I do."

"Did you ever follow up on the story he gave you about being at a meeting?"

"I didn't, and now I regret it."

"You have to follow up today!" she exclaims.

"I plan on it."

"Anybody else?" Mystery asks.

"Something really weird happened at the memorial service yesterday."

"Do tell! I like weird." Clara leans forward, eager to hear the story.

I fill Clara and Mystery in on the drunken debacle that was Ethan.

"You must confront him today, too!" Clara exclaims. Who needs colleagues when you have ghosts to nag you repeatedly?

"I plan to! I'm told he works at the oil change place on 6th Street, so as soon as I finish my bagel and get ready, I'm going over there. I hope he didn't stay home to nurse his hangover!"

21

"Hi Ethan, my name is Holly Daniel. I was at the memorial service yesterday, and I'm a paranormal private investigator."

"You're a what?"

"I'm--"

"Never mind. If you're here to lecture me on my behavior at the memorial service, you can save it. My sister hasn't stopped yammering at me ever since."

"I don't really care so much about what you *did* at the service; it's what you *said*."

"I told everyone yesterday I was joking about killing the chaplain. Sheez, who knew no one in this town could take a joke?"

"So, assuming you didn't kill the chap--"

"I didn't! I just said I didn't!"

"Of course, but I'd still like to know more about your claim that the chaplain talked your mom into giving all her money to him."

"It's no claim, lady. He had her hoodwinked. He's charming and folksy, playing mah jong with the old ladies, eating coleslaw and baked beans. I'm telling you; it was all a front. He was a con artist who bilked the elderly out of their life savings."

"So, you think there were others?"

"Look at the kind of access he had. Old, sick, dying people in the nursing home and the hospital. I bet he has a fortune stashed away somewhere!"

"Can I ask you where you were on Christmas Day? Did you go to the party with the rest of the town?"

"Nope! I was in Texas visiting my in-laws," he insists.

"Do you have some kind of proof?"

"As a matter of fact, I do." He reaches into his back pocket to pull out his wallet. "It's right here. My ticket stub from Frontier Airlines. Flight 502." He shows it to me. "I'm telling you, lady, I didn't kill that guy. But I certainly wasn't sad or surprised to find out someone else did. I bet you that people were lining up to do it. I filed a complaint against him, you know."

"A complaint?"

"Yeah, with the Attorney General's office. So, if a dumb guy like me could do that, you know there have to be others," he offers.

"Good to know; I'll check into it. Thanks for your time."

"Hey, when you find the real killer, tell him I said thanks."

This guy seems mad enough to kill, but his plane ticket is legit. He may be on to something with the complaint, though. If he went to all the trouble of filing something like that, it had to have merit, I'm sure. And if his mom was being swindled, there must be others.

I'm feeling more upbeat than I have since last night. Maybe Ethan is right. There could be a long line of former patients and their families who wanted to kill him.

On the one hand, it's hard to believe that the chaplain was a thief. He seemed like an upstanding guy, and a lot of people clearly loved him. But if what George said about the gambling is true, maybe he stole from patients in the past to pay his gambling debts.

And speaking of George, now it's time to confront *him* about why he lied to Sheriff Mack and me. It would be nice if I could have this wrapped up by lunchtime.

<h1 style="text-align:center">22</h1>

"**W**hat can I get for you, honey?" the waitress asks after I settle into my seat at the counter.

"What's the pie of the day?"

"Cherry," she responds with a smile.

"Fantastic! I'll take a slice with a cup of coffee."

"Comin' right up."

I swivel around in my chair, watching for George. I know he's here because I called first. I hung up before he got to the phone. This isn't a conversation a person has on the phone. Besides, I don't want to tip him off so he can run.

"Is George around?" I ask the waitress as she places the order in front of me. This pie looks delish. For a moment, I almost forget about George, it looks so good.

"He's on break. Do you want me to get him for you?"

"No, that's okay. I'll wait."

"Hey George," I call out with a mouth full of pie, when I spot him about ten minutes later.

"Oh, hey, uh, I'm sorry, I didn't get your name the other day."

"It's Holly."

"When I described you to the sheriff, he said no one in the department matched your description."

My cheeks get warm. Busted.

"He said, and I quote, 'there's a meddlesome private investigator who likes to stick her nose where it doesn't belong who matches that description, however.' You're the meddlesome private investigator, aren't you?"

He leans in close while I swallow a bite of pie in one gulp. But I've come this far. I'll go for it and hope I don't die in the process. "Did you lie to me about what you were doing on Christmas?"

"What do you mean?" he frowns.

I lick my lips. Why is my mouth so dry suddenly? If I stab him with my fork, will that give me enough time to run? I wrap my hand around the silverware. His eyes flick toward the movement. Is it just me, or is it hot in here?

"Several witnesses reported seeing you in an argument with Chaplain Palmer behind the hotel around the time he was killed."

George's hands clench the back of the stool next to me...

He grits his teeth...

All right, Holly, this is it...

Remember, stab first, run second. If you run first, it won't work.

Then, much to my surprise, George sighs heavily, flopping down into the seat next to me. Wait. What's he doing? This isn't how I pictured it.

"Okay, you caught me," he admits.

Well, hallelujah, all I have to do now is call the sheriff, and we can all go home.

"I was at the hotel, and I argued with the chaplain."

"And?" I ask, my fingers still gripping the fork, just in case.

"And that's it. I went to a late-night meeting like I told you earlier."

"After you killed the chaplain, you mean."

"What? No!" he laughs. Why is he laughing? "Did you call my sponsor like I told you to?"

"No," I whisper.

"Well, the sheriff did, and he confirmed that I showed up for the meeting at 10:30, then at 11:30, we came here to get some pie and coffee. We talked for two hours."

That puts him here, eating pie with his sponsor when the chaplain was killed. Rats. Darn these 24-hour diners. I was so sure I had this solved.

"What did you argue with the chaplain about?"

He sighs again. "I stopped by the Christmas party because I wanted to hang out with some old friends. Even though it was hanging with that crowd originally that got me hooked on drugs. I know I'm not supposed to see them, especially on a day like Christmas when everyone is partying, and it's extra hard not to think I can do one tiny little hit, and that's it. I'll be fine. I can control this. But I can't, and the chaplain reminded me of that, so I got mad. He told me to get out of there, call my sponsor, and do a meeting. I was mad, but I knew he was right. I feel like such a jerk because I never got to tell him he was right. Now he's gone, and it's too late."

Then it's my turn to sigh. "I know what that's like."

"George, quit socializing and get back to work!" a man with a cheap tie and wrinkled short-sleeve shirt shouts from across the room. He must be the manager. Why do they always dress so horribly?

"I have to get back to work. But I mean it. Call my sponsor. He'll verify my whereabouts."

"Sure, thanks for letting me know. I'm sorry to have bothered you again." So much for wrapping this up before lunch. Maybe I should order a whole pie and drown my sorrows in sugar and pie crust.

23

My feet crunch on the newly fallen snow as I make my way to the nursing home entrance. Brrr! I rub my mittened hands together. I can't wait to get home, start a fire in the fireplace, and make soup in my Instapot. I found an excellent recipe for French Onion soup on Pinterest that I'm eager to try. I'm so busy daydreaming about delicious soup that I nearly run into a heavily bundled man leaving the nursing home.

"I'm terribly sorry!" I tell him. "I wasn't paying attention."

The man grunts, pulling the hood on his wool coat close to his face as he hurries away. Where have I seen that guy? He looks so familiar.

"Professor Lawson?" I call after his retreating back, but he doesn't even pause. That's weird. I *think* that was him. Maybe he didn't hear me all bundled up like that.

"What can we do for your today?" the receptionist at the front desk asks.

"Am I mistaken, or was that Professor Lawson?"

"Yes, he was here visiting his aunt."

"I thought it was him!"

"Did you need anything else?" she asks.

"Did I what?" Something flits through my brain, but then I'm distracted by why I'm really here.

"I asked if I can do anything else to help you?" the receptionist says, gawking at me like I must be out of my mind.

"Yes, of course. I'm Holly Daniel, I'm a paranormal private investigator, and I'm following up on a lead someone gave me."

"You investigate the paranormal?" the receptionist asks.

"Yes, well, that's my specialty, anyway. The two often overlap."

"Okay. What are you following up on?"

"I'm told that an Ethan Pemberly filed a complaint against this nursing home with the State Attorney General. Who could I talk to about that?"

She makes a face. "Oh, yeah, that guy. If you can wait a moment, I'll contact Human Resources. He'll know what to do."

"Great. Thank you."

"Andy, there's a--" she pauses. "What was your name again?"

"Holly Daniel."

"There's a Holly Daniel here to see you about the complaint that Ethan Pemberly made against us."

She hangs up. For a second, I'm sure she'll tell me that Andy said buzz off, and I don't know what I'll do next.

"Andy Sanchez, our Human Resources manager, will see you. It's the third door to your left." She points down the hallway.

Phew. I was worried there for a second. The more I've thought about it, the more I believe what Ethan said makes sense. If he made a complaint about the chaplain, there must be others. I don't enjoy thinking of the chaplain as a crook, but if he was convincing elderly people to give him money, he'd have way more people hoping for his untimely demise than just Ethan.

The manager's door is open, so I tap on the door frame. He looks up from his paperwork. "Hi, are you Holly?"

"I am."

"Please, have a seat. I'm Andy Sanchez. Our receptionist says you're here about the complaint that Ethan Pemberly filed against the nursing home."

"Yes, I was hoping you'd tell me if there were others."

"Others?" he asks. "Not that I've heard. Why, what are *you* hearing?" He looks worried.

"Ethan told me that the chaplain used undue influence over his elderly mother, convincing her to give him money before she died. He's certain his mom was not the only one and that there would be many others."

Andy shakes his head and groans. "Unfortunately, Mr. Pemberly has been a problem for quite some time."

"I would be too if the nursing home chaplain stole money from my loved one."

"I think you misunderstood. Despite Mr. Pemberly insisting that Chaplain Palmer stole money from his mother, the complaint was quickly dismissed. The nursing home and Chaplain Palmer were completely cleared of all allegations."

"He didn't tell me that."

"I'm sure he didn't. Here, I'll show you."

Andy goes to a large, silver file cabinet in the corner, pulls open a long drawer, then thumbs through the files. "Here it is," he says. "You're welcome to look through it. Don't tell me Mr. Pemberly hired you to investigate this. If he did, I assure you, you're wasting your time."

"No, he didn't hire me. I'm just interested for other reasons." This sounds worse and worse. If it's true, there goes my long list of potential suspects. I flip through the file that Andy handed me. It contains documents showing that Ethan's mother didn't give the *chaplain* her money; she gave it to an orphanage in Zimbabwe. The file Includes a copy of her will and the wire transfer to the orphanage after her estate was settled.

"Between you, me, and the fencepost," Andy says, "Mrs. Pemberly told me that her son was lazy, and her daughter didn't need her money, so she felt her fortune would better serve the orphanage than either of her children."

"Do you know why Ethan said his mom gave the *chaplain* her money when these documents prove it all went to the orphanage?"

"Because Ethan is troubled and angry."

"I'm still confused. Does he know that the money went to Zimbabwe? Perhaps he just *thinks* the chaplain stole it?"

"Nope. Mr. Pemberly has seen every scrap of paper that you now hold in your hands. Unfortunately, he holds a grudge against all involved. He keeps hoping for a big payout, which I assure you will never happen. There's no reason for it."

Then Andy crosses the room to pull a picture off the wall, which he hands to me. "That orphanage was the chaplain's pride and joy. He sent every penny he could raise to it. He told Mrs. Pemberly about it. She decided it was a worthy cause and willed her estate to them." The picture shows a group of children and adults all gathered around a small building in what I assume is Zimbabwe. In the middle of the grinning group is Chaplain Palmer.

"Oh boy," I sigh.

"I take it this isn't good news for you?"

"Forgive me. I mean, it isn't bad news or anything, it just isn't what I was expecting."

"I'm sorry I couldn't be more helpful."

"No, that's okay. You've been plenty helpful. It's not your fault that it wasn't what I anticipated."

I drive home in silence, wondering what to do next. In a few short hours, I've managed to rule out not just George, but an entire list of potential suspects I was imagining in my head. The fact that Gabriel's DNA was found on the chaplain keeps popping back into my head. The more suspects I rule out, the more the evidence points to Gabriel after all. This is a disaster.

24

— · —

When my phone rings, I'm surprised to see it's Gabriel. Is he calling from jail? No. He wouldn't have his cellphone in jail, would he? I'm almost afraid to answer it. Why is he calling?

"Gabriel! How did you get a phone?" Ack! Did I really just say that?

"I'm out on bail," he announces glumly. "Are you busy? Could you stop by the hotel?"

"Oh. Uh. Sure." There go my plans to make soup and curl up in front of the fireplace with a good book.

When I arrive at the hotel, he's waiting for me in the lobby. I follow him into his office, feeling the weight of everyone's eyes on us. They'll be gossiping about this for weeks to come.

"Have a seat, Holly."

I try to think of something appropriate to say. What do you tell someone who was arrested for murder? How was jail? Is it as bad as I've heard? Congratulations on making bail?

Instead, I blurt out, "Did they really find your DNA under the chaplain's fingernails?" Not as smooth as I had hoped, but who has time for small talk?

"That's what they tell me," he says.

"You sound like you don't believe it."

"I swear to you. There is no possible way that my DNA was on the chaplain."

"The medical examiner is lying?" I ask.

"Lying. Mistaken. I don't know. I never touched the chaplain. Much less murder him," he insists.

"So why are you telling me this? Shouldn't you talk to a lawyer?"

"I have. My lawyer says I'm not to discuss this with anyone."

"But you're telling me," I point out.

"I want to hire you."

"Me? But I already work for you!"

"You're a private investigator, aren't you?"

"Well, yes, but..." I hesitate. Now I know where this is going.

"I'll pay you to investigate. I need to find the real murderer because I will not go to jail for something I didn't do while a killer goes free."

He has a point there. What if he didn't do it? Despite the evidence showing he did. That would mean the killer is still roaming the streets of Glenwood, which is a scary thought.

"Truthfully, I'm already investigating this. After someone threw that brick through the window, I decided it was necessary."

"Well, that's great! What have you found?"

This could be a problem. A suspect wants details. Should I share what I've already learned? Even if I doubt that he's the murderer?

I choose my words carefully. "So far, I've only run into dead ends. I just came from the nursing home where I thought I'd find a long list of suspects but came back with zero." He looks so crestfallen my heart hurts. "I'll make you a deal. If I find something I need to ask you about, I will. Otherwise, I'll continue to investigate this like I've been doing."

"You don't believe me," he says resignedly.

"At this point, I'm not sure what to believe. But deep down, I still don't think you killed the chaplain."

"I'll take it. For now, anyway," he says with a small smile.

I truly hope he didn't do it. I'm worried it would be terrible publicity for the hotel, which is just getting back on its feet after the fiasco with the missing tiara. Plus, if he really is a shifter, I don't want to give anyone an easy excuse to use that against him or other paranormally gifted beings. We still don't know who threw the brick through the window, we may never know, but there could be others like that out there.

"I better be going now." I shake my boss's hand for what I hope isn't the last time. "I have a new soup recipe calling my name."

"Of course, of course. I hope I didn't send you too far out of your way."

"No, you're good, and I'll see you at my next shift."

As I make my way out of Gabriel's office and to the front door, I hear a "Pssst!" I look around but see nothing. Did I imagine that? I keep going. "Pssst!" What on earth? Then I see Fiona across the lobby hiding behind an enormous potted fig tree. She waves at me to come closer.

"Why are you hiding?" I ask. "No one can see you but me!"

I pause when she places a finger over her lips, waving me over a second time.

"Fine!" I throw my hands in the air. Ghosts have a flair for the dramatic.

"What is it?" I whisper when I'm right in front of her. I realize how odd I must look when I'm talking to ghosts as it is, but now, to passers-by, I look like I'm having a secret conversation with a fig tree. I know people talk to their plants, but this is a little ridiculous.

"Billy the Bulldozer and his henchmen are in the bar right now," she whispers, as if someone might overhear her.

"Okay."

She blinks back at me wordlessly.

"Is there something else you want to tell me?" I ask, wondering where this is going.

"He's bragging about how he bribed the medical examiner who performed the chaplain's autopsy."

25

"He what?" I shout. "You could have led with that, you know!"

People in the lobby are really gawking at me now, so I wave back like everything is fine. Just lecturing this plant, is all.

"Come with me!" I tell her, reaching for her hand before I remember that it won't work. I'm so excited I've forgotten all the rules. "Never mind. Follow me," I tell her, waving my hand.

I slip into Gabriel's office, slamming the door shut.

"What is it?" he asks in surprise.

"This may seem weird, but just follow along."

"Uhhh, okay."

"I have a ghost here with me."

Fiona waves at him like he can see her.

"She's waving hello."

He then waves into the opposite corner. I would laugh if this wasn't so serious.

"She's actually in the other corner, but whatever..."

He puts his hand down. Embarrassment and confusion cloud his face.

"All right, Fiona, start from the beginning," I tell her.

"Billy and his friends came in earlier than usual this evening."

"So, they got a head start on their drinking?"

"Yes," Fiona says.

"You know I can't hear her, right?" Gabriel asks.

I wave him off. "I'll let you know when we get to the good part."

"Whatever you say." He shrugs.

He won't be shrugging when he hears what Fiona said. Or my translation, anyway.

"As you can imagine, they're extra drunk by now," she continues.

"Of course." I nod.

"They've been boasting about finally getting rid of that," she pauses, then whispers, "shifter."

"He can't hear you," I remind her.

"Oh, that's right."

Gabriel crooks an eyebrow in my direction. "They're bragging about getting rid of you."

"That's it! I've had it!" he shouts, jumping to his feet and slamming his hands on his desk.

"Just hold on," I tell him.

Fiona continues. "They said with him gone, they can take back control like they had when Mr. Sinclair was the manager. Then the fat one who always grabs at the waitresses said, 'That was brilliant, boss, bribing the medical examiner.'"

"Blimey!" I exclaim.

"What?" Gabriel throws his hands up. This must be so frustrating for him.

"Billy bribed the medical examiner."

Gabriel starts for the door.

"Just wait!" I block the doorway. "Let her finish."

He's enraged. I'm sure I'd feel the same way, but we must plan our next move carefully. No telling what these guys will do when confronted. We should call the sheriff's department. Hey, look at me. Sheriff Mack would be proud. Instead of me being the one who has to be talked out of extreme action, I'm the one doing the talking.

"Go on, Fiona."

"Joey asked how he did it. Billy said the medical examiner has a kid with a bad liver and is deeply in debt."

"How would he know that?" I ask.

"Joey asked the same thing. Billy said he knows everything that happens in this town."

"Then what?"

"Billy said the medical examiner caved in minutes. He agreed to alter the DNA results to say they belonged to Gabriel."

My jaw drops in shock.

"What. Is. It." Gabriel grabs my shoulders in desperation. Wow, is he strong.

When I gasp in surprise, he immediately drops his hands. "I'm so sorry. I'm desperate here. What did she just tell you?"

"The medical examiner has a sick kid with medical bills. So, he altered the DNA results to say it was yours."

For a moment, I'm convinced Gabriel will collapse with shock. Or vomit. He went from pale to green and back to pale again.

"Move!" he tells me.

Yikes. He doesn't have to say that twice.

He throws open the door, sending it right through Fiona. Then he storms into the bar, his fists clenched, with me on his heels. I know I should hide and call Sheriff Mack, but after everything we've been through recently, I'm not missing this.

"Bishop!" he barks so loudly that several customers in the bar jump in their seats. When they see his expression, a few of them hurry from the bar. They don't know what's happening and don't want to be here to find out.

"You bribed the medical examiner to frame me for murder?" Gabriel bellows.

After hearing that, the remaining customers sprint from the bar. The ones who thought they wanted to stick around to see what all the excitement was about decided they didn't need *that* kind of excitement.

"How? Who?" Billy sputters, glaring at his friends, who immediately shrug and wave their hands to show they had no part in Gabriel finding out. Their stunned and dumbfounded expressions would be hilarious if this weren't deathly serious. They're used to having the upper hand over everybody else. Not the other way around.

When Gabriel moves toward Billy, I'm sure he'll snap his neck. I watch in horror. I don't want to see this, but I can't look away. Should I call Sheriff Mack? Should I duck or hide? I can't move. I'm frozen to the spot.

But just as Gabriel reaches for him, Billy pulls out a gun. Gabriel then moves in front of me to protect me. See, I knew this guy couldn't be a murderer.

Billy keeps the gun trained on him. "Joey, call the airstrip and tell them to ready the plane. It's time to blow this town."

"Sure thing, boss," Joey says as he calls whoever has this plane Billy mentioned.

Meanwhile, Billy and his henchmen move away from Gabriel, who continues to shield me.

"You think you're so smart," Billy sneers, making a slow, methodical trek to the door.

I can't believe they're getting away with this. Can't anybody stop them? If only Juliet or Wendy was here. They could knock the gun from his hand with a spell. Sometimes, spirit communication is the most useful tool in the world. Others, not so much.

"I don't know how you found out, but you're right. I bribed that idiot medical examiner, and it was so easy. I always make a note of the ones with sick kids. They're the easiest to bribe. I had him switch the DNA results to show that it belonged to Gabriel. I knew they'd arrest *him* for murder, and I'd finally be free of him. Now my plans have changed a little. That's fine. I'm sick of this stupid town, anyway. I'll move on, and you'll never find me."

While Billy and his goons watch Gabriel, afraid of what he might do next, despite Billy having a gun, they don't see Sheriff Mack and several deputies move into place behind them.

The moment he turns around, he's face to face with the cavalry. I wonder how they knew?

"Time's up, Billy the Bulldozer," Sheriff Mack says sarcastically. "Drop the gun and come quietly."

If it were me, I'd drop the gun before the sheriff could finish the sentence, but Billy is such a dimwit he still stands there, pointing the gun at Sheriff Mack's chest. How can the sheriff be so calm when there's a killer with a gun in front of him?

Billy's henchmen, on the other hand, immediately throw their hands high in the air. Maybe they aren't as dumb as I thought.

"Don't do anything stupid, Billy," Sheriff Mack warns. "Just put the gun down nice and easy, and we'll have a friendly conversation down at the sheriff's department. No one else has to get hurt."

Billy shakes his head vigorously. "You'll never take me a--"

Before I can draw another breath, Gabriel is on top of Billy, flattening him. When his gun skitters away, a deputy grabs it, placing it in a side pocket.

I can't believe how fast my boss is! Gabriel's anger and frustration boil as he lands several powerful punches before the deputies can pull him off to handcuff Billy.

"We've got it, Molina!" the sheriff yells at him. "I don't want to arrest you too."

Gabriel finally raises his hands and backs up.

"How did you know we were in trouble?" I ask a deputy.

He shrugs. "The desk clerk called to say he thought something was wrong in the bar."

"Are you okay?" I ask my boss as the deputies lead Billy and his crew from the hotel. Several patrons even applaud them on their way out. "I can't believe that's it. We're done!" I tell Gabriel. I know I said I hoped to have this wrapped up before lunch, but I'll settle for dinner.

"And some people think this town is boring," Gabriel huffs as he tries to catch his breath.

"I never thought that," I laugh.

"I'll be in touch tomorrow to get your statements," Sheriff Mack tells us. He reserves an extra shake of his head just for me, like he can't believe he had to rescue me from this type of situation once again. I'm shocked myself.

26

Once they're gone, Gabriel turns to me. "I think it's time for a celebratory drink."

"Sure! What would you like?" I ask.

"Nope. I'll do the honors. After all, if it weren't for you, we couldn't have caught the killers."

"I'll take that!" I tell him. "Do you know how to mix drinks?"

"I'm a man of many talents," he assures me.

"Then I'd like a daiquiri, barkeep."

"One daiquiri coming right up."

I'm impressed by how deftly my boss mixes our drinks. "Drinks on the house!" he shouts at the people gathered in the lobby peeking into the bar to see if all the excitement is over.

"Yay!" several cheer, filing back into the area. Nothing like free drinks to drum up business.

As he puts the drink in front of me, he says, "Didn't you mention something about making soup for dinner?"

"Oh. Yeah." I laugh. "I forgot all about the soup."

"Are you hungry?"

"Now that you mention it, I'm famished."

Gabriel picks up the phone on the bar top. "Hey Jerry, what's the soup of the day?"

"How about some Chicken and Dumpling soup?" he asks me.

"I'll take it!" I exclaim.

"What else you got?" he asks into the phone.

"You want a monte cristo sandwich with fries?"

"Yes, please!"

"Could you send that over to the bar? Two orders," he tells Jerry. "It's for Holly and me. Thanks."

He hangs up. "Dinner is on the way."

"Thanks!" I tell him.

"Thank *you*," he says, while we clink our glasses together in celebration.

"I knew it was Billy all along," I insist.

"Then why were you at the nursing home looking for a list of names?" he tilts his head at me.

"I always hedge my bets."

"No doubt," he chuckles.

After our delicious dinner and a lively conversation about everything other than catching mobsters, I decline another drink. I have to get home because Clara will be worried as usual and I'm suddenly feeling exhausted. Triumphant but exhausted.

27

— · —

"I dunno, I think she might really be dead this time," Mystery says with her face so close to mine that if she weren't a ghost cat, her whiskers would tickle.

I open one eye. "Still not dead," I grumble.

"Is it true?' Clara asks hopefully.

"It's true," I tell her with a smile. I'm sure she saw the story on the news. "We solved the murder mystery. Billy and the rest of the rotten bunch are in jail. They admitted to bribing the medical examiner to alter the DNA results."

"That's fabulous!" she exclaims.

"Now we need to find that dang peridot before the mayor alters *my* DNA," I tell them.

"Oh dear, I'd almost forgotten about that," she fusses.

When the doorbell rings, we look at each other in confusion.

"Who is ringing the doorbell this time of the morning?"

"Maybe it's Sheriff Mack!" Clara says.

"Ugh. I hope not. He never has good news, does he? What time is it, anyway?" I ask, glancing at my bedside clock.

"Maybe it's someone with Girl Scout cookies!" Mystery exclaims.

"At 7 AM in December? I don't think so."

I slide my feet into my fuzzy bunny slippers, throw on my robe, then head down the creaky stairs.

"Keep your shirt on!" I shout when the doorbell rings again. I swear if this is a salesman, I'll slam the door in his face.

When I open the door, I'm stunned to see Mayor Gill on my doorstep. She does not look happy. Don't get me wrong. She's dressed to perfection, as always. Her closely cropped silver hair is perfectly coifed. Her makeup is on point, with nary a lash out of place. Her designer pantsuit is without a single wrinkle. How does she do that? But her expression is anything but pleasant.

She thrusts today's newspaper in my face, forcing me to stare at the front page. It's a picture of the sheriff's department leading Billy and the others away in handcuffs, along with Gabriel seething with me peeking out from behind him. I have got to stop getting my picture in the newspaper.

"Oh, look! There you are again!" Clara squeals, pointing at me. Fortunately, the mayor can't hear that. I doubt she'd be as excited as Clara.

"Now that you've solved the murder case, can you please find my Precious Peridot?" she says, testily.

"Would you like to come in for coffee, Mayor Gill?" I ask.

"I don't have time. Just get my peridot!" she barks, shoving the paper into my hands. Then she spins on her heel and stomps back to the waiting town car.

"Good morning to you, too," I mutter, thumbing through the newspaper on my way to the kitchen to make coffee.

"Boy, are you in trouble!" Mystery whistles.

"She's right. I swore I'd find the peridot before New Year's Day, but I got so involved in the murder mystery that I pretty much forgot about it."

"You talked to that professor," Clara reminds me.

"Actually, I need to check back in with him. I want to follow up to see if he's had news about anyone trying to sell it."

"You helped put a murderer in jail yesterday. You need some breakfast before you solve another case. It's the most important meal of the day, you know," Clara tells me.

"Clara, what would I do without you?" I chuckle.

After breakfast and a shower, I head to the college in my obnoxiously pink, fully restored 1960s VW Bus. The previous owners abandoned it at the house because they thought it was haunted.

It is.

We're not sure how or why, but Clara and Mystery can ride in the bus. They just can't get out unless we're at home. The previous owners took it for a test drive one day while working on it, and unknowingly took Clara, who happened to be in the back seat, for a ride. Even she didn't realize she could ride in it.

She was so excited to realize she was in the bus while it was moving, she jumped up and down, kicking the back of the driver's seat. They couldn't hear her, but they could feel her.

They already knew a ghost was haunting the house. The fact she could haunt the bus as well was the final straw. They sold the house and left the car behind. I would never purposely choose a vehicle like this, but when my old Subie died on the second day in Glenwood, I had no other choice.

It annoyed me to no end in the beginning the way everyone in town waved at me like I was in a parade. I even threatened to paint it beige. But eventually, I came to enjoy it. It's quite the adventure.

I park the bus in the guest parking lot and head inside. When I reach the geology department, I realize I should have called first. I don't even know if the professor is in today.

"Hello, excuse me. Is Professor Lawson in today?" I ask his young secretary, who barely bothers to look up from the game she's playing on her phone.

"He's out at the moment. He's in a faculty meeting. You can leave a note for him on his desk if you want," she tells me.

"I'll do that. Thanks."

I stroll into his office when I unexpectedly catch the name on the door: H. Jonas Lawson. I pause. "Excuse me, what does the H stand for?"

"Herbert."

"Herbert? That's an old-fashioned name," I tell her.

"Right? I'd go by my middle name too, if I were him."

The nagging recollection I had at the nursing home yesterday, right before it slipped away, sneaks back into my thoughts. Professor Lawson told me he'd never been to the nursing home. But yesterday, the receptionist told me he often visits his aunt who lives there.

Could it be Mildred? It must be! She asked if I'd seen Herbert! That has to be him. Why would he lie to me about that? Is he embarrassed? He shouldn't be embarrassed just because she has Alzheimers. Maybe he didn't want his personal life made public. That's so weird. But whatever. People are strange. Especially these ivory tower types. I have more important matters to worry about at this point.

I take in his disorganized office, wondering where I'll find a piece of paper and a pen. I try to avoid rifling through his things, but it's hard not to. Finally, I locate what appears to be a piece of scratch paper and a pen.

Hello, Professor Lawson! I have some follow-up questions about the missing peridot. Have you heard anything? Let me know when you're free to talk. Thanks! Holly.

I place the note and pen in the center of his desk where, hopefully, he'll see it when he gets back. When I turn to leave, my scarf gets caught on a stack of files, knocking them to the ground. Fiddlesticks! I can't take myself anywhere.

I bend down to pick up the files while trying to organize them a little before putting them back. But when I stand up, a crumpled sheet of paper flutters to the ground. What the heck is wrong with me? This office is messy enough. I don't need to add to it.

As I reach for the paper, my eyes land on the excruciatingly tidy handwriting. It's written in blue ink, and the letters are unusually uniform and neat. He can't keep his desk clean, but he can write this neatly?

To whom it may concern,

Let this letter serve as my confession in the event of my untimely demise. I fear my life is in danger at the hands of a local mafia gang.

Was the mafia after the professor too? What did they want with him? Whatever it was, he can rest easy today. You're welcome, Professor.

I know I should put this back without reading further, but I can't help myself. How often do you come across a letter like this?

As many people in this town know, I've devoted much of my life to my beloved orphanage in Zimbabwe.

Wait, what? Was the professor involved with an orphanage, too? How many orphanages are there in Zimbabwe?

Last summer, damage from an earthquake threatened the orphanage unless they raised crucial funds for repairs. Funds in an amount that I had no hope of raising. So I did something I'll regret for the rest of my life, however long that may be. I stole the Precious Peridot.

The room spins. My heart races so fast that I feel dizzy. I plop down into the professor's chair.

I hoped to sell it on the black market, but it disappeared before I could sell. I don't know what happened to it, but I fear it's gone forever. I'm so very sorry.

Sincerely, Chaplain Christopher Palmer

I clap my hand over my mouth to keep from shouting, *Chaplain Palmer?* My hands shake uncontrollably. Why does Professor Lawson have this letter?

He told me he didn't know Chaplain Palmer and that he'd never been in the nursing home. This is all just so bizarre. I feel sick.

The chaplain stole the peridot? How is that even possible? If I ever thought I would have a panic attack, it's now.

"Is everything all right in there?" the receptionist calls out.

She startles me so that I nearly drop the letter. I forgot she was out there.

Then I do something that's either incredibly brilliant or incredibly stupid. I'm not sure which. I grab the letter, fold it, stick it down my shirt, then book it out of Professor Lawson's office.

"Have a nice day!" the secretary says as I sprint down the hall.

28

I run to my bus, not knowing what to do next. Think, Holly, think. If there's one thing I've learned since moving here, it's when in doubt, turn to friends you can trust, so I text Wendy and Juliet.

Meet me at the bakery in five minutes. Emergency!

What have you done now, Holly?

Are you being held hostage?

No!

As I pull out of the campus parking lot, my phone rings. It's Sheriff Mack! Isn't that a happy coincidence?

Before I can say a word, he says, "Holly, I called to let you know you need to watch your back. After interrogating the medical examiner, we discovered that the DNA we found under the chaplain's fingernails wasn't in our database. That means the killer couldn't have been Billy or his men."

"How do you know that?"

They've been arrested so many times their DNA has been on file for years."

When I realize what that could mean, my heart pounds even faster.

"Uhhh, Sheriff?"

"I'm not going to like this, am I?" he groans.

"Probably not. But I need you to meet me at Sol Conceptions Bakery in about five minutes."

"Have you been kidnapped?" he asks.

"No."

"Are you being held at gunpoint?"

"No." Why do they keep asking that? That only happened once. Or maybe twice. Kind of.

I can *feel* his exasperation. "I'll see you there in five."

Thankfully, there's a parking spot available in front of the bakery. I breathe a sigh of relief, leap from the bus and run inside. The others are already there, so I flip the sign to close, then lock the door.

"Whoa, this is serious," Juliet says.

"You guys will never believe what I just discovered," I announce breathlessly.

When I reach into my shirt, the sheriff mutters, "uh oh" under his breath.

I brandish the now extra crumpled letter at them. Sheriff Mack snatches the paper from my hand while Juliet and Wendy squeeze in next to him so they can read together.

"Where did you get this?" Wendy asks.

"That's the crazy part," I tell them. "I found it in Professor Lawson's office."

"Who's Professor Lawson?" Juliet asks.

"He's a geology professor at Colorado Mountain College. I've been consulting with him about the peridot."

"How did *he* get this letter?" Sheriff Mack asks.

"No clue!"

"You didn't ask?"

"Uhhh."

"You stole this from the professor?" Sheriff Mack says.

"Uhhh."

"Does he know you have it?" Juliet asks.

"I don't think so." Why are they giving *me* the third degree? "When I went to see him, his secretary barely looked at me. I don't think she could describe me if she had to. And I didn't give her my name."

"Well, thank goodness for that!" she exclaims.

"Did the professor ever mention a connection to the chaplain? Did the chaplain give him this for safekeeping, perhaps? And then you stole it?" Wendy suggests.

"No! When I first met the professor, he lied about the nursing home and the chaplain!" I'm so wound up; it's all just spilling out of me. But I forgot the others don't know this part of the story.

As patiently as I can, I fill them in on my theory that Mildred, from the nursing home, is Professor Lawson's aunt. What I don't understand, though, is why he lied about it.

"The chaplain wrote in the letter that the peridot disappeared. Do you think the professor stole it?" Wendy asks.

"No, because he was out of the country the entire time. His office confirmed that when I called last summer."

"This is so confusing," Juliet says, shaking her head.

"You think this is confusing? Tell them about the DNA," I point to Sheriff Mack.

"The medical examiner said the DNA didn't belong to any of the mobsters," he tells them.

"So, you don't think they killed the chaplain?" Wendy gasps.

"Nope!"

"Oh great. That means they're out of jail?" she says.

"Oh no, it's still illegal to bribe a public official. They'll be in prison for a long time for that. But now we need to find out how the professor got that letter." He points at me. "I meant what I said. Be careful. I'll have a patrol car drive by your house every hour to monitor the situation."

"I'm sure I'll be fine. But thank you," I tell him.

<h1 style="text-align:center">29</h1>

I arrive home to find Clara waving at me from the front yard. What is that silly ghost up to now? When I pull into the garage, she zooms in beside the bus. She must have seen something good on the news. Maybe the sheriff already picked up Professor Lawson.

However, as I close the garage door, Professor Lawson steps out from behind one of the storage units. He's holding the note I left for him in the middle of his desk. Boy, do I feel dumb.

"It would have taken me a lot longer to figure out who took the chaplain's letter if you hadn't so conveniently left a calling card," he says with a sneer.

He doesn't appear to have any weapons, but I don't think I have a chance against him, given his size. I also realize at that moment that he's big enough to have strangled Chaplain Palmer.

I step out of the bus slowly while hoping to plot my next move.

"Hand over your phone," he demands. I give it to him reluctantly. There goes that plan. I hoped to sneak an emergency call when he wasn't looking. He glances at it. "Wendy wants to know if you got home all right. Not really!" he laughs, stuffing it in his back pocket.

"Gimme my letter!" he says.

"It's not your letter," I remind him.

"Well, it isn't yours either! Now, where is it?"

"I swear I don't have it anymore."

"Then where is it?"

I pause, hoping to invent a good story on the fly.

"You took it to the police, didn't you?" He shakes his head in disgust. "Why did you have to go and do that? If you had just kept it, you could have handed it over, I'd go on my merry way, and all would be fine."

"You don't believe that any more than I do," I scoff. "You plan to kill me no matter what."

"So you aren't quite as dumb as I thought."

I shrug. Is that a compliment? Probably not.

"Holly! I tried to warn you not to pull into the garage!" Clara cries.

"I know. I didn't realize what you were doing until it was too late."

"I tried like the dickens to move this shovel enough to hit him with it, but it's too heavy."

"It's not your fault, Clara."

"Who are you talking to?" Professor Lawson asks.

"Nobody. Just the voices in my head," I tell him, hoping if he thinks I'm crazy, he'll get scared and leave. It's worked before, right?

He tilts his head like he's pondering something. "No, that's not it. You're a spirit communicator. You see dead people! Aunt Milly mentioned she talked to you at the memorial service, and I thought she was spewing nonsense as usual. But now I get it!"

"I thought you didn't believe in that sort of thing."

"I was raised in a paranormal family. Why do you think I became a scientist? It was the ultimate rebellion for me to insist it was all hogwash."

"I can't believe you were raised in a family like that."

"Aunt Milly is a direct descendent of the original coven that gave that the peridot to Glenwood. I'm practically paranormal royalty around here."

When he pauses to plot his next move, I calculate whether I could beat him to the shovel sitting in the corner.

"Hang on a second," he says suddenly. "If you can talk to dead people, you can talk to spirits at the nursing home." When I don't respond, he laughs. "Don't even try to deny it. I know you can. Get back in the bus."

"Why?" Is he going to kill me in it? That doesn't make sense. Yet all these horrifying thoughts go through my head.

"We're going to the nursing home."

Huh? Does he plan to kill me in the nursing home?

"I need you to question the ghosts to see if they know where the Precious Peridot is."

Rats. Even I didn't think of that.

On the way to the nursing home, I imagine a dozen moves I could make to throw him off his game. I could wreck the bus. But that might kill me in the process. I could flip off a passing cop car. Of course, I'll never see one when I need one. But you know what? The weird part of me wants to find out if the spirits really do know where the peridot is. Hopefully, I can think of a way to save myself after that.

"Can I ask you a question?" I glance at him, assuming he'll never answer, but what the heck, might as well give it a shot.

"You want to know how I got the chaplain's letter?"

I nod.

"I got it when I went to see my aunt a couple of weeks ago after returning to the US. She didn't know who I was, but that's not unusual. She has her lucid moments, although those are fewer and further between these days. But just as I arrived, I saw the chaplain was leaving--"

"Hang on a second. The first time we met, you told me you came back on Christmas Day," I point out.

"I lied. Duh. But as I was saying, the chaplain seemed edgy, like he was in a hurry. Didn't even say hello." He holds his hand up when I start to interrupt again. "Yes, I lied about knowing the chaplain as well. He brushed by me in the corridor and hurried on. The letter you found in my office," he nods at me, "fell out of his Bible. I called out to him, but he kept going; he was in such a daze. I picked it up, intending to leave it at the front desk. But I couldn't help myself. I had to read it. I am a curious scientist, after all."

I roll my eyes. Yes, that's the important part of his story. The fact he's a scientist.

"When I read the letter, you can imagine how shocked I was. I put two and two together and realized the chaplain must know who my aunt is. She probably told him on one of her good days. When I confronted him that night behind the hotel, he admitted to taking her on a field trip to the museum, hoping when she saw the gem, it would trigger something in her memory."

"He needed her to lift the spell," I point out.

"Apparently, it worked. They pocketed the peridot and went back to the nursing home. When I confronted him behind the hotel on Christmas, he told me thought it would be safe hidden in Aunt Millie's room."

"But you told me you didn't believe in the spell, or was that a lie too?"

"I don't believe in it. But the chaplain and my aunt do, so that's what counts."

"But where in her room did he hide it?" I ask eagerly. This is it. We're getting the peridot back.

He shakes his head. "He didn't say. He just told me when he returned to claim it, it was gone. And before you get too excited, believe me. I've searched her room from top to bottom. It isn't there. My guess is someone who works at the nursing home discovered and took it."

Wonderful. We're back to square one. It could be long gone by now.

"Did you ask your aunt about it?"

"I've asked her repeatedly. She doesn't remember."

"Why did you kill him?" I ask. "I mean, obviously you did. It's the only thing that fits."

"I didn't mean to. I just wanted to scare him. I was so sure he was lying about losing it. I thought he was waiting for the right moment to sell it. I just couldn't believe that anyone would be dumb enough to leave something that valuable with an old woman with serious memory issues. Turns out the chaplain wasn't the smartest criminal."

"According to Sheriff Mack, most of them aren't. Why would he confess all of this to you? It's not like you were good friends. Why should I believe you after all this time?" I ask.

"That guy was so wracked with guilt he would have confessed to a turnip if he thought it would listen."

"You obviously wanted the peridot for yourself. What were you planning to do with it? Sell it, I assume?"

"Oh no! Not at all! I wanted to be the hero. I wanted to be the one who rescued the town by finding the missing peridot. Think of the things that I could get from that. Department chairmanship. All the grants I could ever want. Publishing houses would fight over my story--"

"You did this for nothing but prestige?" I interrupt.

"What do you mean, nothing? It would have been everything," he sighs.

When we arrive at the nursing home and enter the building, Professor Lawson squeezes me tight around my shoulders.

"If you say anything to anyone, I'll snap your neck on the spot," he tells me.

Eww. I don't think he's actually capable of that. It can't be that easy. But I also don't think I'm willing to take that chance just yet.

I'm desperately hoping the receptionist realizes something is up and contacts the authorities. There must be a way to tip someone off. I'm crushed to discover that no one is at the front desk.

"Where's the best place for you to summon the spirits or whatever it is you do?" he asks.

"I don't summon them. I just see them wherever they happen to be. Like the living. Except not."

He loops his arm around my neck. I try not to panic, but this is nerve wracking and uncomfortable.

"Where did you see ghosts when you were here for the memorial service?" he asks.

"There were quite a few in the rec room where they had the reception."

"Great. Rec room it is."

There has to be a pile of people in the rec room. This will be my best chance. What are the odds if I make my move on the professor to bring him down that the elderly residents will join in? With enough of us I think we can prevail.

Why are the halls so quiet? All the doors are closed and there's no staff around. Where the heck is everybody? No cops on the road, no patients or staff lingering in the hallway. I swear I have the worst luck.

When we enter the rec room, there isn't a single living person in there. This is bizarre.

"Do you see any ghosts?" he asks. "And don't lie to me!" he warns, further tightening his grip around my neck.

"There's a man in the corner."

"Ask him if he knows anything about the peridot!" he demands, releasing his grip on me, shoving me in the direction I just pointed.

I wasn't lying to him. There really is a ghost in the corner. He's sitting in a chair staring into space as if he's daydreaming. I suppose ghosts can daydream too.

He pushed me so hard that I stumble and nearly fall. When I try to regain my balance, I hear a gunshot. Oh no! He has a gun and he's shooting at me.

Wait, no, it's not a gunshot. It's a heavy door slamming shut. I whirl around in the noise's direction.

It's Sheriff Mack, several deputies, Wendy and Juliet. Yes!

"Don't move!" the sheriff growls, his gun steadied in Professor Lawson's direction.

But how did they know?

"You called them!" Professor Lawson accuses me like I'm the bad guy here.

"How would I call them? You have my phone!" I remind him.

As the deputy handcuffs him, Wendy jumps forward to snatch the phone from his pocket.

"Actually, your butt called me," she says, laughing at him.

"Your text!" I exclaim.

"We heard every word!" Juliet says.

"You were making fun of the text she sent me, but when you put it in your pocket, it must have accidentally called her."

Wendy nods vigorously. "We got here first and cleared everyone out so they'd be safe. Then we waited."

"You guys are the best!" I grin at them. "Even you, sheriff."

"Save the family reunion for another time. We need to get this guy to the station," the sheriff grumbles. Perhaps I should have thanked him first. When we file out of the rec room, the residents and staff begin to appear, hoping the coast is clear so they get to see what the fuss is about.

But just as they start to take him away, Mildred rushes up to us. Oh, dear. I hoped to avoid this. What if she recognizes her nephew and doesn't understand why he's being arrested? What will we say to her?

"You came back!" Mildred says, recognition filling her face. It takes me a moment to realize she's talking to me and not her nephew.

"I did."

"I told you I had something special for you."

Could it be? Could it possibly be? But I'm crushed when she holds out her empty fist like before. I knew it was too good to be true. But I play along once again by holding out my hand because I feel for her. I hope she doesn't realize they just arrested her nephew for murder.

She holds her fist over my hand.

I'm stunned when she drops a small wooden box into my outstretched palm.

"This is for me?"

She nods excitedly.

I try to open the box, but there's no visible lid. Oh great. It's one of those puzzle boxes. I am the worst at puzzles. I've always said I could never be on the tv show Survivor because I'd be eliminated the first day by my inability to solve even the simplest of puzzles. Sure, I can solve mysteries, but a physical puzzle? Nope!

"I'm sorry. I don't know how to open this."

Now Mildred looks confused again. Uh oh. I think we've lost her.

"What do you think?" I ask, handing the box over to Juliet. "Please tell me it isn't magic. Or if it is that you have a spell to open it."

Juliet holds the box quietly. "This was sealed with powerful magic."

Oh great.

"Excuse me, nurse?" Mildred calls out. "When's lunch?"

I can't believe this. Mildred may have just handed us the Precious Peridot. Missing for months and who so many think caused the town's misfortune, but we can't get at it because it's locked in a magic box by someone who may or may not remember her own name. I want to cry.

Suddenly Mildred turns to me. "No need to cry. Come, child," she says beckoning to me with gnarled fingers. Juliet hands the box back to me, then Mildred gently takes it from my outstretched hand.

She murmurs words I've never heard. I look to Juliet and Wendy, hoping it will sound familiar, but they shrug in ignorance. Mildred's idiotic nephew looks like he's about ready to cry himself. Good. He'll be crying for a long time where he's going.

After she completes her incantation, she puts her thumb on top of the box, sliding the lid off. She nods at me, so I hold out my hand once again and I swear I stop breathing. How long can a person go like that? Seconds? Minutes? She tips the box, and a gleaming, awe-inspiring, 304-carat peridot gem drops into my hand. No one makes a sound. We all stare at it in wonder.

"Can I hold it? Pretty please?" Professor Lawson begs. "You promised you'd ask!"

"Get him out of here!" Sheriff Mack barks at his deputies.

30

5 ...4...3...2...1 Happy New Year! Everyone cheers when the clock strikes midnight. The Red Castle Hotel put together a last-minute bash to celebrate the recent success of recovering the Precious Peridot. It's back in its proper place at the museum. This time guarded by a pressure-sensitive alarm. You know, just in case.

In one of her more lucid moments, Mildred assured us that her coven's protection still stands, though. Unless she decides to steal it again, she said. She thought that was hilarious. The museum curator and the mayor, not so much.

"Hey there, George!" I greet my former murder suspect.

"Happy New Year!"

"What are your plans for the new year?" I ask him.

"I have some exciting news. Several high schools in the mountain range have asked me to come and talk to the students about how drugs nearly ruined my life before I turned things around. I'm even going back to school myself this spring. I'm going to become a social worker."

"That's great!" I tell him, reaching up to hug him. "I think the kids will really relate to you."

"Chaplain Palmer's death has left a big void, so I'm hoping to help in any way I can."

"I don't doubt that the kids and their parents will be grateful for your story."

"Great party, girlfriend!" Wendy exclaims, bounding up to me. "And Happy New Year!" She raises her glass.

"Don't tell me more peppermint martinis?" I groan.

"Nope! I'm sticking with ginger ale tonight. I've had my fill of peppermint martinis until next Christmas."

"Good plan. You should thank Gabriel for the party. It was all his idea. I just went along with it."

"Yes, but thanks to you, the Precious Peridot was recovered, and business today was better than it's been in months."

"And you think it's because the peridot is back in its proper spot?"

"Don't knock the magic. I'm just glad that everything can get back to normal now."

"My friend, if you're happy, I'm happy."

As I scan the room of joyful revelers, I marvel at the fact that only a week ago the peridot was still missing, and Chaplain Palmer was alive. You never know what will happen when you wake up in the morning, do you?

"So, what are your plans for the new year, young lady? Anything exciting?" Gabriel asks.

"I moved to Glenwood less than a year ago and have had enough excitement to last me several. So, no, I have no exciting plans. Quite the opposite. How about anything *but* exciting?"

"You know you just cursed yourself, right?" he says.

"You'd think I'd learn, wouldn't you?" I sigh.

Ghostly Glenwood Mysteries Paranormal Cozy Mysteries

The Case of the Haunted Hotel

The Case of the Pilfering Poltergeist

The Case of the Poached Peridot

The Case of the Gym Ghost

Marcall's Breakfast Cafe Paranormal Cozy Mysteries

An Eggscellent Day for Murder

24 Carrot Caper

Daggers and Donuts

Cupcakes and Corpses

A Crime of Cranberry

Peppermints & Pandemonium

Star Spangled Homicide

Blood Curdling Ballots

Sign up for my email list here

https://mailchi.mp/9ebce0da866a/email-signup-list

Visit my website

biskinnerauthor.com

Follow me on Instagram **@bethiskinner** Facebook **@biskinnerauthor**